SURRENDER

FEMME & DOMME
EROTICA
BOOK 1.

Chaya Clemmons

"I was in bloom, susceptible, open, flower-like."
- Anaïs Nin, from a diary entry in *Mirages: The Unexpurgated Diary; 1939-1947*

Surrender

Femme & Domme Erotica

Beautiful and bookish lawyer Anja Sonnen's life changes forever after she meets her new client, Madison Fabre - sexy, intelligent and dangerous.

Anja had in mind a plea bargain but Madison has a secret line of defense - turning her attorney, the prosecutor, and the judge into her submissive personal pets.

For information on hot new releases and a free erotica ebook subscribe to

2

CHAPTER 1. APPOINTMENT

After three years as a prosecutor in the New York County District Attorney's Office and two years as a defense attorney at the Law Offices of Baum and Meyer, Anja Sonnen felt that nothing would surprise her. Baum and Meyer was a boutique law firm targetting the legal needs of wealthy individuals. Anja had been specifically recruited to help them respond to the legal needs of a particular class of wealthy person – those who considered that the rules did not apply to them.

Madison Fabre was not what Anja Sonnen had pictured in her mind when she read the prosecution brief. Madison had somehow managed to avoid the news photographers wanting to catch a photograph of who the journalists described as the spider at the center of the lesbian sex scandal web. The story had been the central focus of the news over the last few days.

Madison was stunningly beautiful with dark mesmerizing eyes, Vietnamese and French heritage, and walked with straight-backed elegance. As Madison sat down opposite her across the shiny boardroom table, Anja could not help but notice Madison's slender curves in her tight-fitting houndstooth skirt and white blouse. Madison's shiny black hair was pulled together at the back with a black ribbon.

"I have been sounding out Sonya Petersen, the DA, in relation to a plea bargain," Anja said.

Madison looked out the large arch window of the boardroom at the art deco building outside.

"It's beautiful outside today," said Madison, " Can we discuss the case outside?"

"Your dime," said Anja.

They grabbed takeaway coffee at the local Starbucks then walked to Central Park and then along the Bethesda Terrace.

"Are you interested in reaching a deal with the DA?" Anja asked.

"I am pleading not guilty," said Madison.

"You know the case against you is strong."

"I'm quietly confident," Madison said with a smile that indicated that Madison knew something that Anja did not.

As they went deeper into the park, they found a quiet park bench under a tree, surrounded by ornate flowering bushes. It was there that Madison removed Anja's glasses and kissed her gently on the lips.

"Madison, it is inappropriate for a lawyer to ..."

Before Anja could finish her sentence Madison kissed her again, firmer and more passionately this time, first on the lips then down along Anja's neck. Anja took a deep breath. Madison wrapped her hand out behind Anja's head and stretching her fingers through Anja's hair, massaging the back of her head as she kissed Anja. Madison then placed her hands on either side of Anja's face and kissed her face with such softness that everything else faded from Anja's mind. There was nothing else. Just these kisses. Just this moment.

Madison then unzipped the back of Anja's dress down to midway down her back. Madison kissed Anja again along her neck so that Anja almost swooned with delight while at the same time looking around nervously to see if anyone could see them.

Madison pulled the top of Anja's dress down over her shoulders and kissed each shoulder in turn as Anja closed her eyes. Madison then pressed her lips onto Anja's forehead, breathing in her musky perfume.

"You smell good," Madison said looking Anja in the eyes. Madison smelled to Anja like someone she once knew.

"So do you," Anja said, moving her hand over Madison's cheek, her skin soft and smooth.

Madison looked into Anja's eyes. Anja moved her hand behind Madison's head and pulled her towards her lips, stroking the back of her head as she breathed Madison into her, tilting her head back slightly as they kissed. Madison's fingers untangled the nerves in Anja's head as they pulled Anja deeper into the kiss with Madison. Anja forgot they were in the park as everyone else and everything else just faded into the background. It was like Madison had the key that unlocked Anja's pleasure.

Madison's hand clasped the small of Anja's back and she pulled her even closer. Madison's other hand teased along Anja's leg and the hem of her dress.

Madison then peeled off Anja's dress without saying a word. They kissed for what seemed to Anja to be an eternity, a fire burning from within her, pulsing along her veins. She could feel the fire within Madison as well, a powerful force pressing against her ready to explode.

Madison removed Anja's bra and kissed each of her nipples and then said, "Remove your panties please Anja."

Anja looked around the park nervously. *What if someone saw me? Someone from work?* Thankfully there was no one in sight.

Anja slowly grabbed the waistband of her panties and looked at Madison as she edged them down her trembling thighs.

"Good girl," said Madison as she stroked Anja's nipples and held them, firm buds between her fingers, "Open your legs slightly."

Anja again looked around nervously and slightly parted her legs, the park bench cold beneath her.

Madison reached down between Anja's legs and traced a finger with great care along Anja's slit. Madison then dipped her middle finger between the folds and stroked very gently up and down. When Madison received a gush of approval she studied Anja's face, her skin was flushed, her eyes closed in pleasure. Madison then traced small circles around Anja's throbbing clit, gradually adding more pressure. Anja gave a desperate moan. When Anja opened her eyes they were watery. and she looked so vulnerable.

Anja rested her head on Madison's shoulder. She was so soft, so vulnerable and naked against Madison. Anja gave herself over to Madison completely.

"Please put your fingers back in," said Anja, almost pleading.

Madison slipped her fingers back between Anja's legs. Anja was dripping with desire.

"Oh, Madison. That feels so good," Anja sighed, not being able to completely give herself over to pleasure while having to make sure that no one could see them.

"Anja, I want you to lick my shoe," said Madison.

The request was so strange to Anja. It did not make sense but the feeling of desire for Madison was so strong.

"If it would make you happy," Anja found herself saying.

"Ms. Fabre," Madison corrected.

"If it would make you happy, Ms. Fabre," Anja said with a shy smile.

Anja again checked to see if any passersby could observe them and then bent down to the pebbled ground and delicately kissed Madison's shiny high heeled shoe. Madison ran her hands through Anja's blonde hair, massaging her scalp.

"And the other shoe," said Madison, softly but firmly.

Anja putting the small O of her mouth around the tip of Madison's shoe. Just the slightest touch of her lips against the tip of Madison's shoe made Madison feel more aroused, wanting so much more but not wanting to push Anja too far on a first date.

"Lick it," said Madison.

Anja checked again for passersby and then leaned forward on her knees and stroked Madison's shoe with her delicate pink tongue. Anja then looked up at Madison's face which was slightly flushed with pleasure.

Anja moved her mouth over the top of Madison's shiny black shoe. Anja moved her mouth over the top of it. Anja's lips pressed against the coldness of the shoes leaving a light trail of kisses. Anja felt intoxicated by her desire for Madison. Anja just did not care that they were in Central Park. She felt an almost dangerous compulsion to do whatever would please Madison.

Madison continued stroking the back of Anja's head and when Anja looked back up at Madison her eyes were closed, lost in the moment. Madison then looked down at Anja and smiled, "Anja, go and stand next to that tree over there."

Anja looked around again. She could see a couple walking in the distance but there was no one who could see them. Anja stood naked up against the tree, opposite to where the couple was. Anja's sex was a pink camellia with her lips being soft petals.

"Tell me what you want, Anja," Madison said.

Anja sighed and purred, "I want you inside me."

"Show me where you want me, Anja," Madison said.

"Yes, Ms. Fabre," Anja said, using two fingers to open herself revealing the pink, soft-skinned core of the flower.

Anja turned to look at Madison and smiled with delight. Every sense in Anja's body was focused on Madison as she approached with something dark in her hands. Madison placed one hand on Anja's buttocks and smiled as she pulled Anja's body towards her, entering Anja with something solid, black and rubbery.

Anja looked into Madison's eyes as she moved the object within her. Madison thrust into Anja firmly, Anja's back rubbed up against the bark of the tree. Madison moved her right hand from Anja's buttock and started to stroke between her legs as she continued to thrust into her, circling her clitoris with her thumb. Madison then lifted her hand to caress Anja's face then kissed her deeply as the intensity of the thrusting with the object increased with Anja's hips gyrating and the tremors of her pleasure increasing in intensity.

The kiss stifled an involuntary moan from Anja as she felt the delicious pressure released from between her legs, through her clitoris and tingle along her back and throughout her body.

CHAPTER 2. OFFICE

The next morning Anja stared at the pile of files in her in-tray that needed attention but her thoughts kept coming back to her new client Madison.

Anja pulled out Madison's file and read through the prosecution brief, trying to reconcile what was in there with the Madison she had met the day before. Anja had never felt such a strong attraction to another person before.

She could not believe what had happened in Central Park. Could it be that Madison had this crazy effect on everyone who fell into her orbit? Perhaps that's what explained all the events described in the prosecution brief.

Anja thought about transferring Madison's case to someone else. She knew it was highly unethical to have a relationship with a client and already her objectivity was completely out the window.

The best outcome Madison could get would be through doing a deal with the DA but that would still mean Madison going away for a few years. The alternative was facing trial and with such a strong prosecution case, a conviction was inevitable as was a much longer prison sentence. Anja tried to push the thought of it out of her mind and kept reading over the telephone number for Madison in the inside cover of the file.

Madison's iPhone vibrated with a new message on the small café table at Savoureux, next to an expresso and baguette. Madison glanced at the telephone but then returned to watching Sonya Petersen, who like herself was dining alone.

Sonya was reading the New York Times which she had to fold due to the smallness of the tables at the café. Sonya smiled at the waitress when she placed her order and Madison noticed how Sonya's eyes followed the waitress as she headed to the kitchen. The waitress did look amazing. That was part of the reason it was Madison's favorite place for breakfast.

The waitress was Renée Mercier, a French actress, fresh from drama school in Paris, who had already obtained some smaller roles in Broadway shows and currently had a role in Les Misérables. Sonya's face lit up again when Renée came back with her order.

"Merci," said Sonya, briefly exchanging smiles with Renée before she moved to take orders at another table.

Madison returned to the message on her telephone from Anja and tapped a reply with one hand while sipping her coffee with the other – "I can be at your office in five minutes."

"No problem. I'll see you soon," the reply popped onto Madison's screen.

"Ms. Fabre, good to see you again," said Anja shaking Madison's hand in front of Anja's secretary.

As soon as Anja's secretary had closed the door to the meeting room, Madison brought her other hand up and stroked Anja's cheek, barely touching the skin.

Anja gestured to one of the chairs, "Please take a seat."

"Thank you," said Madison.

"I have been thinking about what happened yesterday and have decided it would be best if you obtained alternative counsel."

"No. I want you. You are the best," said Madison.

"Ms. Fabre, don't you see – if we are in a relationship my objectivity and your interests are compromised," said Anja glancing at Madison but then looking away, not wanting to be distracted by her beauty.

"What underwear are you wearing today?" asked Madison.

"Don't change the subject," said Anja.

"You don't have to tell me. Just spread your legs under the table," said Madison as if her request was perfectly normal and acceptable.

Anja looked at the door of the meeting room and then at Madison then slowly parted her legs slightly, just enough to give Madison a glimpse of her black La Perla panties. Anja was surprised by how ready she was to obey and push to one side who she thought she was.

Did Anja need the directness of Madison to silence her inner turmoil? The brutal truth was that Anja was simply aching to be intimate with Madison again.

Anja parted her legs further. Madison looked under the table.

"Nice. But I have bought you something better," said Madison, opening her handbag and bringing out a purple package and sliding it across the boardroom table.

"Thank you but can we go back to working out your representation now?" Anja said placing her legs firmly together.

"Aren't you even going to open it?" Madison asked with a mischievous smile.

Anja opened the package and examined the contents – silk stockings, a garter belt, and black but sheer panties and bra.

"They would go so well with those high heels you are wearing," Madison said.

Anja shifted uncomfortably in her chair.

"Stand by the window and hitch up your dress," whispered Madison.

Anja looked to the door again and then as if she was hypnotized walked to the window and lifted the hem of her dress with one hand.

Madison came in close and looked at Anja's face, flushed with passion and placed a finger at the bridge of Anja's crotch and rubbed it back and forth slightly and then showed Anja the glistening finger.

"Are you always so wet?" Madison asked.

"Only for you Ms. Fabre," Anja replied.

"Taste it," Madison commanded.

Anja opened her mouth and Madison placed her finger in. Anja sucked upon the finger with her eyes fixed on the door of the meeting room. *There is no explanation for what was going on here*, she thought.

Bridget removed her finger from Anja's mouth and then pulled Anja closer, stroked her cheek with the back of her hand then moved the hand along the side of Anja's breast.

Madison then held Anja's waist for a moment with both hands and pulled her closer before kissing her softly for a moment, her lips barely touching Anja's lips.

Madison then slipped her hands under Anja's dress to hold Anja's bottom. Madison looked into Anja's eyes. Anja's face was full of desire.

"I would love to parade you around the office in your new lingerie," Madison whispered in Anja's ear then kissed Anja softly on the cheek.

"I don't think that's a good idea," Anja whispered back, her heartbeat thumping.

"At least put them on for me. At $500 per hour that's the least you can do for me," said Madison.

Anja smiled slightly, "It's your dime, Ms. Fabre."

Anja then nervously removed her clothing, every sense heightened watching the door and listening for movement. Her secretary knew not to disturb her during client appointments.

Madison watched closely, button by button and the undoing of zips before Anja was completely naked.

"Now put on your new lingerie and stand facing the window," Madison whispered into Anja's ear.

Anja followed Madison's instructions then turned around to see Madison removing her skirt.

"Did I say, you could turn around, Anja?" Madison said sternly.

"Sorry Ms. Fabre," said Anja, turning to face the corner of the room again as Madison opened the box to reveal a black double-headed strap on dildo. Madison then pulled her black panties down over her black stockings, licked her fingers and then lubricated herself between the legs and eased one end of the dildo into herself and tied the straps of the dildo around her waist.

Madison walked over to Anja who was still stroking herself between her legs.

"OK Anja, now I'll guide the dildo between your legs," Madison said, "Take as much as you can."

As Anja guided the dildo Madison thrust forward into Anja who found the sensation incredible, a shiver going down her spine. The feeling of warm euphoria built within. Her heart was racing.

"I've been thinking of you constantly since yesterday," Anja said, turning her head to see Madison.

"Eyes forward Anja," Madison said, thrusting deeply into Anja.

"I don't know what's come over me," said Anja, slightly breathless as Madison kissed along her neck, lighting little fires, while her fingers gripped Madison's muscular shoulders.

The muscles in Madison's arms tensed against Anja as she lifted her up and down upon her dildo.

Madison enjoyed forcing Anja up against the window, her pale skin flushed pink.

Madison then grabbed hold of Anja's long blonde hair and held it forcing her head slightly back as she thrust into her. Madison then raised her hand in the air and smacked Anja's pale buttocks with her hand, leaving bright pink marks as she continued to ride her.

"What do you say, Anja?"

"More please," Anja said breathlessly.

"More please, what?" Madison said sternly.

"More please, Ms. Fabre," Anja said on the verge of orgasm.

Madison then slapped Anja on the buttocks again making a loud slap. Anja wondered for a moment whether the other lawyers might here them.

Madison then brought two slaps down on Anja's buttocks in quick succession. Anja's head hung low, her long blonde hair falling over her face.

Madison withdrew and said, "Show me, Anja."

Anja then reached around and parted her sex with two fingers.

Madison lent down and studied Anja. She was so wet and quivering.

Madison slipped a finger between Anja's legs and gently massaged her inner thighs and gradually moved in and rubbed either side of Anja's clit until she could hear her sigh. She then reached between her legs and grabbed between them, making her arch her back and stand on tippy toes.

"What would you like me to do?" Madison whispered in Anja's ear.

"Please take me again, Ms. Fabre. I'm yours," Anja said looking Madison intensely in the eyes.

Madison removed her hand and edged the dildo up between Anja's legs, rocking gently between them at first, and then edging in bit by bit with each thrust, grabbing Anja's red buttocks for leverage. Madison slid the dildo to and fro within Anja, bringing it deeper into her while simultaneously rubbing upon Anja's moist nub. Anja was penetrated so deeply she had to stand on tippy toes with Madison's breasts pushed so close to Anja's back that she could hear Madison's heart, perfectly synchronized with her own.

Madison found Anja was so wet and inviting, thrusting her body backward and forwards on the dildo, her body moving with Madison's body in perfect harmony. Anja sighed at the delicious fullness between her legs, the soft bergamot smell of Madison, her ardent thrusting, her sighs and finally the release as Anja quivers from each spasm, giving herself over to the wildness, the animal passion, the storm.

That night before falling asleep Anja thought of Madison with her eyes closed.

In her mind, Anja used her hand to trace the sides of Madison's face, her nose and trace around her mysterious smile and her almond eyes. Madison's face seemed to Anja so close and intimate to her but also in another sense distant and unknowable.

Anja kept the image of Madison's face in her mind until it faded into sleep.

CHAPTER 3. MAISON

The following day Anja arranged to meet Madison at her house, a mansion in upstate New York with a large brick fence and ornate black gate which Madison referred to as 'La Maison'. It was also the location from which the prosecution alleged Madison had conducted the alleged lesbian sex cult from which her charges had arisen.

Anja was greeted at the door by a maid. Inside La Maison was muted lighting, dark leather Chesterfield couches, elaborate flower arrangements in blue and white china vases. She had lunch in the dining room with Madison. The meal was beautifully presented with excellent wine. On one wall was a large aquarium with brightly colored tropical fish and the other wall had large windows with a magnificent view of the grounds.

After they had finished their meals Anja leaned over and kissed Madison who then whispered, "Take off your shirt and wrap it around your eyes to make a blindfold."

Anja looked around, "Ms. Fabre, what if the maid comes back?"

"Chloe knows me very well. There is nothing that would shock her. Believe me," Madison said, "Now, are you going to be a good kitten and do what I say or you will have to be punished?"

Anja looked around again and then gingerly pulled off her shirt and tied it around her head. Anja wondered who she really was any more. It was if she had removed the photograph of herself from the frame and she was not sure what was replacing it.

"Very good, kitten," Madison said, "Now slip out of your bra, dress, and panties and put your panties in your mouth."

Anja quickly followed Madison's instructions and soon stood pale, naked, blindfolded, gagged and fragile in the dining room.

"Now on the floor," Madison said and Anja crouched down to the floor.

"Get down on all fours," Madison commanded.

"Arch your back," Madison said, "OK, up, now down."

"OK, put your head down, low to the ground and your bottom up high."

Anja started to worry again about the maid coming into the dining room.

"What if..." Anja mumbled through the panties.

"Did I say you could talk?" Madison said, spanking Anja's buttocks with her hand, leaving a slight redness on Anja's milky white skin.

Madison pulled up a chair and sat admiring Anja.

Madison studied every curve and crevice of Anja as if she was a foreign landscape.

Madison traced her finger down the nape of Anja's neck, along her spine and between her legs, stopping to play with Madison's fingers were damp and Anja's clitoris stood proud. Madison bent down and massaged it with her tongue, flicking back and forth. Anja sighed.

"Did I tell you that you could make a noise?" Madison chastised her.

Anja bit her lip.

Madison gently rubbed either side of Anja's clitoris with her fingers then returned to licking it and then gently sucking upon it until it was a hard little nub.

While sucking, Madison reached around with her hands and massaged Anja's breasts and held her nipples and gently pulled them until they were also standing proud and hard.

Madison then stood up and walked around Anja.

Anja felt something cold around her neck which clicked together at the back.

"What's that?" Anja tried to say through the panties in her mouth.

"It's a pearl necklace but no peeking for now," Madison said, her breath heavy, her hand stroking along Anja's bare leg.

"OK. Let's go for a walk," Madison said.

Madison held a long pearl rope which led to a pearl necklace around Anja's neck.

Madison pulled on the rope and Anja crawled on the wooden dining room floor as Madison led Anja in a circle, enjoying the sway of her bottom and breasts as she moved.

Madison then led Anja back to the dining table and removed the pearl necklace from around her neck.

"Move yourself up onto the table and lie on the center of the table," Madison commanded.

Anja lay down as instructed.

"Legs far apart please, Anja. Wider please," Madison said.

Anja spread her legs as far apart as she could.

"Good girl," Madison said, "Now open your lips with your fingers."

Anja used two fingers to hold her labia apart so Madison could see deep within her. Madison examined Anja from every angle.

"Very good. Now use one hand to play with your breasts and your other one to play with your clit. That's it. You need to be good and wet for what I have in mind."

Madison watched Anja writhing in the center of the table, stroking her breasts and stroking between her legs, studying what gave her pleasure.

"I'll be back. Don't stop. But don't orgasm either," Madison said leaving the dining room and going to her study.

Madison switched on her computer to search the internet on the prosecutor, Sonya Petersen and her previous cases on the computer for fifteen minutes. She had prosecuted many of the high profile cases that had made the headlines.

Madison then slipped back into the private dining room where Anja was still stroking herself with a look of complete intensity in her face.

Chloe came into the dining room with two glasses of champagne.

"Don't stop," Madison said as Anja sat up looking embarrassed.

"Thank you," said Madison, sipping the champagne as Anja lay on the table and resumed stroking herself.

"How much am I paying you per hour, Anja?"

"Oh...oh...$500 per hour," said Anja.

"Worth every cent," said Madison.

"Oh," Anja sighed on the brink of orgasm.

"Stop!" Madison commanded in a way that gave Anja a shock, "Now stand up, hands behind your head."

Madison felt between Anja's legs and rubbed her fingers together, "Very good."

Madison then picked up the pearl necklace and rope and hooked one end of it onto a picture hook on one side of the dining room and hooked the other end to another hook on the other side of the room.

"Now stand either side of the pearls, still with your arms above your head and walk from the middle to the end of the pearls."

Anja lifted her leg over the middle of the pearl rope so that it brushed against her leg.

"Move forward," Madison said.

Anja stepped forward and the pearls rubbed against her thigh.

"And again," Madison said.

Anja stepped forward and the pearls glanced against her inner thigh.

"And again," Madison said.

Ther time the pearls just touched the outer lips of Anja's sex, smooth and cold.

"And again," Madison said.

The pearls were now deeply between Anja's legs. Madison held the pearls on either side of Anja and moved them back and forth.

"And again," Madison said.

Anja now had to stand on her toes; the pearls were tightly between her legs, penetrating deeply between her lips.

Madison stroked Anja's breasts and then tweaked her nipples before kissing along her neck.

"One more step and you are there," Madison said.

Anja stood forward. She was now standing high on her toes.

Madison brushed either side of Anja's stomach with the back of her hand.

"You did well Anja," Madison kissed Anja's cheek while stroking Anja's buttocks.

Madison then unhooked the pearl necklace.

"OK, Anja. You did so well at that task. I am pleased with you but have another task for you. Hands behind your back," Madison said, removing the panties from Anja's mouth.

"Yes, Ms. Fabre," Anja said with her head bowed, her fingers interlocked behind her back as Madison wrapped the pearl necklace around her wrists binding them together.

Madison then sat upon the dining table and unbuttoned her blouse and removed it then her bra then nodded to Anja.

Anja leaned forward and licked the side of Madison's breasts in long licks and then kissed and sucked upon Madison's nipples until they were hard nubs. Madison tipped her head back in pleasure with her eyes closed.

"Follow me," Madison said, leading Anja out of the dining room by the pearl necklace which still bound her hands behind her back.

They walked past Chloe and Anja's eyes briefly met Chloe's eyes before returning to looking at the wooden floor.

Madison led Anja up a flight of stairs to her bedroom and then to a large bathroom where Madison turned on the shower and soon the room was filled with steam.

"Anja now kneel in the shower and wait for me," Madison said.

Anja followed this instruction. The hot spray of water fell upon her as she knelt, waiting patiently as Madison removed her skirt and panties.

Madison entered the shower recess, holding a large rubber dildo like a truncheon.

Anja immediately moved her head forward between Madison's legs. Madison was so aroused that she received Anja's tongue immediately deeply within her then Anja's quick tongue encircled Madison's clitoris before she sucked the gentle nub as hot steamy water fell upon them.

"Stand up Anja," Madison said breathlessly.

Anja looked up at Madison and nodded. They stood eye to eye. Anja wanted desperately to be kissed by Madison whose lips lingered close to Anja's lips.

Madison whispered, "Lean up against the glass."

Anja stepped away from Madison and leaned her head and breasts against the glass of the shower recess. It was then that she noticed that Chloe was in the bathroom sitting on a chair watching them.

"I hope you don't mind. I asked Chloe to watch us," Madison said.

Madison then edged the dildo up between Anja's legs. It slid into Anja easily despite the size of it. Slowly Madison thrust into Anja, efficiently but sensuously as Anja's breasts pressed against the glass of the shower recess. Madison penetrated Anja deeper and deeper, Anja's legs trembled and she closed her eyes as Madison kissed the back of her neck.

CHAPTER 4. SAVOUREUX

The following day was a warm June morning. Madison felt incredibly content. She sent her lawyer home and caught a taxi to Savoureux for breakfast and managed to score a seat by the window with the bright sunlight falling upon her copy of the New York Times where she was reading the latest theatre reviews.

Fortuitously Sonya Petersen happened to be sitting at the adjoining table.

"Les Misérables has been getting very good reviews. Have you seen it?" said Madison.

Sonya looked up from tapping on her telephone, "Sorry, do I know you?"

"Oh, I've just seen you here before. I think for both of us this is our favorite café," Madison said, smiling.

"Well yes. It is very pleasant," Sonya said.

"I'm Maddy," said Madison holding out her hand.

"Sonya."

They shook hands and Sonya was about to return to her telephone when Madison said, "Did you know the waitress from here is in the show - Renée Mercier – she's playing Fantine."

"I didn't know that," Sonya said, looking more interested.

"Renée goes to the same gym as me. She gave me two complimentary tickets to the show but all my girlfriends are busy tonight," said Madison.

"That's a shame," Sonya said.

"Would you like to come with me? It would be a waste to not have someone use the ticket."

"Oh, thank you but I couldn't impose on you like that."

"It's no trouble, really. I've arranged to meet Renée before the performance. She would be disappointed if I did not use both tickets."

"What time is the show?" Sonya asked.

"We could meet in the foyer at 7 pm," Madison said.

Sonya smiled, "You know what. I would love to do that. I'll see you then."

"Done," smiled Madison.

When Madison arrived at her office she spent her PA into a spin, arranging to get two tickets to the very popular Broadway show and arranging a meeting with Renée Mercier in her dressing room before the show. Luckily for Madison, her PA was just as persuasive as Madison herself.

Sonya waved to Madison in the foyer at the Majestic, dripping in jewelry

"Sonya, you look amazing," said Madison, "Come follow me. Let's go see Renée."

One of Madison's talents was that she seemed to instinctively be able to find places and never got lost. They walked with such confidence past the security man at the Majestic that he did not even think to challenge them on why they were heading off to the change rooms.

"Have you seen, Renée?" Madison asked one of the actors as they passed.

"The last change room on the left," the man pointed.

Madison knocked on the door and immediately entered with Sonya in tow. Renée was sitting in her nineteenth-century underwear, and checking her makeup in a lighted mirror.

"Renée, how are you?" Madison said, approaching Renée and kissing her on both cheeks.

"Hello, how are you? So glad you could make it tonight," Renée said.

"This is my friend Sonya," said Madison.

"Sonya, from the café. So glad you could make it too," said Renée, kissing Sonya on the cheek.

"Our pleasure," said Sonya, "Are you all ready?"

"Oh, I'm feeling nervous, to be honest. Last night I stumbled on the dialogue and am worried about doing it again."

"You need to relax, Renée," Madison said, "Hop up onto that sofa over there, lie down on your front and I'll give you a quick massage to relax your muscles."

"OK, just for a minute. I'll need to get into my dress soon," said Renée lying down on the couch.

Both Madison and Sonya took a second to take in the absolute beauty of Renée.

Madison massaged Renée's upper back in concentric circles.

"Sonya, can you do the other side, while I do this side?" Madison asked.

Sonya approached, somewhat nervously, "Oh, I don't know. I'm not in the habit of giving massages."

"Come on, it's easy. Just do what I do," said Madison.

Sonya then massaged the other side of Renée's back.

"Oh, that feels so good," said Renée.

"You're letting all that tension built up in your back out," said Madison.

"OK, now the lower back," said Madison, now massaging in concentric circles in the lower back region, Sonya joining her on the other side.

"Now the buttocks," said Madison.

"Wow, that is amazing," said Renée.

"Now the legs," said Madison as each masseur massaged the legs in concentric circles.

"Can you turn around for me, Renée?" asked Madison.

Renée shuffled around onto her back on the couch, her eyes closed.

"OK, now let's do the temples. Very gently," said Madison.

"Now the chest," said Madison who noticed that Renée was starting to get aroused by the sign of her nipples pressing hard against the nineteenth-century underwear.

Sonya had noticed as well and was almost dizzy with pleasure watching Renée lie there.

Madison noticed that Sonya was almost salivating over Renée.

"Renée, would it be OK if Sonya kissed you?" Madison asked.

Sonya interjected, "Oh no. That wouldn't be right, Maddy."

"Sure, she can kiss me," said Renée.

Sonya drew breath, both excited and confused. She looked down upon Renée who was now looking directly into Sonya's eyes.

"But make it quick. I really do need to get dressed," said Renée.

Sonya smiled with a twinkle in her eye and maintaining eye contact gently pressed her lips against Renée's lips.

Sonya found Renée's lips soft and felt for a moment that she was melting into her.

Sonya then kissed along Renée's neck, tentatively at first and then more confidently.

Madison silently photographed the couple with her mobile phone before slipping it back into her handbag.

CHAPTER 5. WILD

Madison printed the photographs of Sonya Petersen and placed them in a folder with the tickets to the Majestic. She then filed the folder under "S" in her home office filing cabinet and locked it.

It was a Saturday and she drove to Anja's building and collected Anja from the street.

Madison was pleased that Anja was wearing a retro empire dress with her hair up as instructed.

They drove out of New York to Eagle Rock Reservation. Anja was impressed by the immaculate white Cadillac SUV that Madison was driving.

Anja wound down the window and the wind rushed through her hair as the stereo system pumped with Beyoncé's Homecoming album.

Madison eventually drove the car off the main road down a small lane that went through the forest and parked next to a stream that was dappled with sunlight passing through the leaves of the surrounding trees.

"Anja, you take the picnic basket and rug and set it up next to the stream," Madison said.

Anja laid the tartan picnic rug down on the soft grass next to the stream and placed the picnic basket next to it. Madison had packed the picnic basket and Anja found the items within it somewhat strange. There was a can of shaving cream, an old-style razor, a blindfold and silver handcuffs.

Madison walked over while Anja was still examining the items and said, "You know how much I love seeing your body."

Anja nodded.

"Do you trust me, Anja?"

"Yes, Ms. Fabre."

"Lie down on the picnic blanket and hike your dress up."

Madison was pleased with the sight of Anja's white cotton panties.

"Now put on the blindfold. Good. Now lastly click those handcuffs into place."

Anja could not find the handcuffs with the blindfold on and so Madison assisted her by clicking one handcuff into place and then another.

Anja felt Madison's hand briefly glance along the crotch of her panties and then felt something hard against her labia. Anja then felt one side of her panties lifted up and was then cut, followed by the other side then the panties being pulled away.

"Now Anja, I would like to give you a shave."

Anja nodded, "Yes, Ms. Fabre."

Anja could hear the spray of the shaving foam and then felt it on her private parts – initially cold and smooth.

Madison caressed the cream over pubic hair and all over Anja's vulva in a manner that made Anja release an involuntary sigh.

"This will be a little cold," Madison said and then Anja felt the cold blade of the razor against her skin and the gentle sweep of it against her skin, removing her pubic hair.

"Spread your legs for me, Anja."

Anja moved one leg out and then another and felt fully exposed as Brigid shaved around her pubic area.

"You are very beautiful," said Madison, " You would look amazing lying on the bonnet of the Cadillac," Madison said, "I could drive you around spread-eagled on the bonnet so everyone could see my beautiful hood ornament."

Anja laughed nervously.

"You think I am joking?" Madison laughed.

Anja felt both thrilled and terrified at the thought.

"I don't think that's a good idea."

Anja then felt Madison's finger on her lip.

"Open," Madison said.

Anja opened her mouth and Madison slipped two fingers into Anja's mouth, moving them in and out of her mouth.

"Make my fingers good and wet Anja."

Madison removed her fingers from Anja's mouth and moved the wet fingers up and down along between Anja's legs.

"What would you like me to do, Anja?" Madison asked showing Anja the wet fingers.

"I want you inside me," said Anja slightly breathlessly.

"How do you address me, Anja?" said Madison stopping the stroking.

"I want you inside me, Ms. Fabre."

"I believe a degree of formality is proper between a lawyer and her client," said Madison, "Now tell me again what you want."

"Please Ms. Fabre, I want your fingers inside me," Anja said feeling a delicious mix of shame and pleasure.

"Well if you want my fingers inside you open your legs wider," said Madison

Anja opened her legs as far as she could. Madison looked at the pink lipped oyster presented to her and brushed the back of her hand between Anja's legs.

"Who does this belong to?" Madison asked.

"It is all yours, Ms. Fabre," replied Anja.

"Anja, now stand up."

After Anja was standing Madison slipped her hand up Anja's dress and left it there between her thighs.

"Come on Anja. I don't want to do all the work," said Madison and Anja started to grind herself against Madison's hand.

"Anja you're not working hard enough," Madison chastised Anja, "Now turn around and bend over."

When Anja was bending over, Madison lifted up Anja's dress to reveal her two bare butt cheeks and with the other hand smacked each buttock in turn.

Two hikers walked along on the other side of the stream. The two hikers, a man, and a woman, both bird watchers, walked along the stream, the man staring at the two young lovers making out so blatantly in broad daylight. The woman elbowed the man in the ribs to break his stare before they walked off.

"Now turn and face me and let's try again," said Madison.

"Yes, Ms. Fabre. I will do better," said Anja, her head bowed.

Madison again moved her hand up Anja's dress and placed it between her thighs. This time Anja ground herself against Madison's hand and arm in a raunchy debauched manner until Madison's arm was slick with Anja's arousal.

Madison then kissed Anja's lips. Madison's lips were tender but her mouth was demanding, her tongue pushing forward to meet Anja's tongue. Madison's hands stroke on either side of Anja's stomach then cups each of Anja's buttocks as Madison continued to kiss Anja in such a passionate way it was as if Madison wanted to consume Anja, her mouth catching Anja's moans as Anja tips over the edge of pleasure. Anja's crotch pulsed against Madison's hand as Madison rubbed the swelling, sensitive bud between Anja's legs. Madison looks deep into Anja's eyes as the pressure builds.

"Oh, I'm going to come," said Anja whose face is flushed and pleading.

"What are the magic words?" asked Madison.

"Please, may I come, Ms. Fabre?"

"You may."

Anja's whole body trembles. Every sense dances with pleasure.

When it is over Anja smiles at Madison, content and satiated. Madison runs her fingers through Anja's blond hair.

"Good girl."

CHAPTER 6. SALON

The next day Madison had invited both Sonya and Renée to lunch at a rooftop Vietnamese garden restaurant named Le salon de Saigon which had dramatic views over New York City.

Madison knew the owner very well and they were seated in a private dining area surrounded by sandstone, cypress, and lemongrass.

Renée arrived looking effortlessly beautiful, braless under a ruffled white blouse. Sonya was the last to arrive, looking slightly hurried.

"Hello ladies," Sonya said before kissing both Madison and Renée on the cheek, "Sorry I'm late. The traffic was crazy. Have you ordered? I'm famished."

"I can order if you like," said Madison who caught the eye of a waitress and ordered in Vietnamese without looking at the menu.

"That was impressive," said Renée.

"I learned Vietnamese from my mother so I could communicate with my grandparents," said Madison.

"My parents and grandparents tell me I now speak French with a New York accent," Renée said.

"I love your accent," said Sonya.

"Merci," said Renée with a little smile.

The food arrived quickly as did the French wine. A total of three bottles were consumed.

"Really I shouldn't have anymore," said Sonya, putting her hand over the top of her wine glass, "I have a hearing at 3.30pm."

"I'll drink it," said Renée with a giggle.

"I have a better idea," said Madison, "Unbutton your shirt Renée."

Renée looked surprised and giggled. Madison wondered if she was ready for the challenge she had in mind. There was an awkward silence and then Renée's hand went up to her blouse and she looked at the other two women and smiled shyly before unbuttoning the blouse so it hung loosely on her shoulders.

Madison then picked up the wine glass and drizzled a few drops of wine over Renée's nipples.

"Sure I cannot tempt you, Sonya?" Madison said as Renée's rosy nipples stiffened.

"You two are scandalous," said Sonya who looked around to check no one was watching and then lowered her mouth to Renée's right nipple and licked it and then her left.

Renée's nipples now pointed upward and her eyes were closed, lost in the moment.

"Renée, lift up that dress of yours and spread your legs," said Madison.

Renée kept her eyes closed but smiled a wicked smile, pulled up her long dress and spread her legs. She was not wearing any underwear.

Sonya's face flushed with desire.

Madison poured the wine so that it went over Renée's pubic hair, between her legs and then pooled on the floor.

"Sonya, get down between Renée's legs and drink," Madison said.

"Oh ladies, this is really too much," Sonya said, looking around but they still had the dining area to themselves. Sonya stared at Renée's beauty and the soft wet cleft between her legs. *How can I resist?* Sonya thought.

Sonya hiked up her tight work dress slightly to allow herself to kneel down and placed her mouth between Renée's legs as Madison poured wine over Renée creating a small waterfall which was falling into Sonya's mouth.

When the glass was drained, Madison said, "Now lick every last drop up."

Sonya licked between Renée's legs, using her tongue to probe deeply to get every last drop of the wine. Renée tilted her head back and placed her feet on the table, either side of Sonya's head.

Madison stood up and watched over Sonya lovingly attending to Renée's pleasure.

"How sweet," said Madison who then without warning, flicked the long white serviette, so that the tip of it struck Sonya's bent bottom like a whip.

"Ouch," said Sonya looking up for a moment.

"Please don't stop," purred Renée.

This was all the encouragement Sonya needed as she more ardently attended to Renée.

Madison again flicked the serviette against Sonya's round bottom but Sonya did not look up this time.

"Sonya, go deeper with your tongue," said Madison.

The waiter came back around the corner but when she saw what was going on, doubled back. Madison noticed the waiter retreating and smiled.

Renée was obviously on the verge of orgasm but Madison was not over her fun and games just yet.

"OK Sonya, hold for a moment," said Madison.

"No, please," said Renée, "Just a minute more."

"Sonya will come back to you," said Madison, "But first she has to strip – just your skirt, blouse, and underwear – leave your heels on. I like how they make you look."

Sonya glanced at her watch and you could see her mind ticking for a moment before she decided to proceed and unzipped her skirt and stepped out of it and then undid her blouse and removed her bra, releasing her fulsome breasts.

"And your panties," said Madison who could see that the panties were soaked with Sonya's arousal.

Madison removed the plates and cutlery from the table and then said, "Renée remove your clothes as well and lie down on the table."

When Renée had done what Madison had asked, Madison said, "Now Sonya, face Renée and interlock your legs with hers," Madison said.

Soon both women were perched on the white table cloth, their legs interlocked and their vulvas pressed against each other, the majestic city skyline of New York behind them.

"Now grind," said Madison.

Sonya and Renée then started grinding together as they kissed each other, releasing soft moans as they pressed against each other.

"Because you are both my special friends, I have got you both a present," said Madison, taking two double-headed dildos out of her handbag. The second one was connected to a belt.

"Now both of you get on all fours and press your bottom against the other's bottom," said Madison.

When the women were in place, Madison eased one end of one dildo into Sonya and then the other end into Renée and then moved the dildo forward and back against the two women, going slightly deeper with each thrust.

"Now you keep this in yourselves," said Madison. The women thrust the dildo between them in rhythm, Renée and Sonya both whimpering with pleasure.

Madison then walked in front of Sonya, strapped the dildo to herself and pressed it against Sonya's cheek and said: "Open up, Sonya."

Sonya then wrapped her mouth around the dildo, pushing it towards Madison with her mouth as she thrust forward.

Madison held the dildo with one hand and with the other hand pinched and twisted Sonya's nipples.

Renée released a sigh as the dildo between her and Sonya slithered with arousal, taking even more of it than she had in the past.

Renée's face had a look of intense pleasure before she released a small cry of orgasm.

CHAPTER 7. JURY

The following day the grand jury was sitting in Madison's case in the New York County Supreme Court.

Madison walked close to Anja as they walked up to the steps to the imposing Roman columns of the courthouse. She was slightly concerned with what security would see in her handbag when x rayed but the security man did not say anything.

"Who is prosecuting today?" asked Madison.

"Charles Watkins – he's fairly new to the DA's office," answered Anja.

What's happened to Sonya? wondered Madison.

Charles Watkins was efficient and to the point as a prosecutor. Anja barely asked a question.

Witness after witness got up before the grand jury and said their piece. Madison had to fight to suppress a smile during the proceedings.

During the mid-morning break, Anja said: "You seem to be enjoying this."

"I am," said Madison as they all walked to an interview room at the court, "It puts me in the mood."

"How do you explain all these women and what they say about you?" asked Anja.

"Regret," said Madison, "But I have learned to live without regret."

"What do you mean?" Anja asked.

"Let's have sex," said Madison, kissing Anja's cheek, leaving a smear of red lipstick.

"Are you mad? The grand jury will be back in a few minutes."

Madison then gently guided Anja's hand onto the soft fabric of her blouse. Anja felt the hard nub of Madison's nipples.

"You are enjoying this," Anja said rubbing Madison's breast slightly with her hand.

"Anja, just take your top off while you do that," said Madison, "Come on, you said we have a few minutes."

Anja gave a doubtful smile then removed her jacket and unbuttoned her blouse.

"Good girl," Madison whispered.

Anja felt a mixture of dread and excitement and it was strangely arousing for her.

Madison then said, "Lean over the desk over there."

Anja gave Madison a look like she was crazy but then quietly went over to the interview desk and leaned over it, her breasts pressing against the cold wood.

Madison approached the desk and moved her hand over each buttock presented to her then with each hand raised the hem of Anja's dress and then pulled down her panties to her knees.

Madison studied Anja, "You do have a very cute butt,"

"Thank you," said Anja, her face as flushed as her buttocks.

"Pleasure yourself," said Madison, pulling a chair up close to Anja's bottom.

Anja's fingers reached down between her legs and shyly moved up and down between her legs.

Without warning, Madison smacked her hand across Anja's buttocks.

"What was that for?" Anja said turning to face Madison.

"Your efforts were half-hearted. When I say pleasure yourself, I mean it," Madison said.

"I was," said Anja, turning to face the wall again, hoping that no one would barge into the interview room.

"You need to go deeper," Madison said, moving two fingers deep within Anja to reach her G spot.

The force of Madison's penetration made Anja move onto her toes.

"You are so tight," said Madison.

A powerful moan came from Anja as Madison pumped her fingers into Anja, making her body rock back and forth against the desk, moving in and out of her.

Then the stimulation became too much as Anja pulsed with pleasure, the danger and vibration causing one of the most powerful orgasms she had ever experienced with wave after wave of pleasure falling upon her and she felt lighter than air. Anja could scarcely breathe as Madison kissed Anja's mouth.

Anja found that she was much more relaxed during the rest of the grand jury proceedings. Madison had a slight smile on the edge of her lips as the jury announced that they were committing her for trial.

CHAPTER 8.
EXERCISE

In the afternoon Madison went to her gym and did a combat fitness class that involved a punishing routine of planks, push-ups, spin, and step.

Madison nodded to Renée who was doing the same class.

After the class, the two women headed to the change rooms.

"It's pretty intense isn't it," said Renée.

"I love it," said Madison.

Madison stared into Renée's eyes and then looked at her lips and slightly leaned in.

"I love your freckles," said Madison.

"Your skin is flawless," said Renée who moved so close to Madison that she could feel Renée's breathe on her cheek.

Madison then curled her hand around Renée's neck and sensuously kissed her on the mouth.

"We should take this somewhere private," said Renée.

"Where?" whispered Madison.

"Well, I need a shower. What about you?" said Renée stripping off her gym wear and leaving a trail of clothes to the shower cubicle, her body gorgeous in every detail.

Madison stripped, then wrapped her towel around her and walked over to the showers. Hot steam was emanating from the shower cubicle Renée was in. She was singing some beautiful song in French that sounded like a lullaby.

As Madison approached the cubicle door opened and Renée wrapped her arms around Madison, her towel falling to the ground and they were wrapped in a naked embrace, Renée's body dressed in steam, warm and inviting.

Renée and Madison consumed each other with their mouths, their tongues intertwined and their hands exploring each curve of each other.

Renée then kissed along Madison's neck, then along the side of each breast, then in a circle around her stomach and then Renée separated Madison's labia to expose the pink orchid within.

The shower spray fell upon Madison's flower then Renée probed her deeply with her tongue while stimulating her clitoris with two fingers.

Madison threw her head back and moaned as Renée grabbed each of her buttocks and held her close. Renée now was probing Madison deeply with her fingers, curling them up while sucking upon Madison's clit. Madison reached down and caressed and stroked Renée's head.

Renée looked up at Madison whose eyes were closed, lost in the moment.

Madison thought she would faint with pleasure as she came, warm nectar between her legs. Renée stood up and cupped Madison's face with her hands and kissed her mouth, her breath hot and her mouth wet with desire.

When they finally separated to draw breath, Renée asked, "Is there something else I can do for you?"

Madison kissed Renée's cheek and said, "Hmm, let me think."

Renée kissed Madison and said, "There must be something."

"I know," said Madison, "I want you to go get your towel but don't dry yourself off. I like you wet. Do you have an iPod?"

"Yes," answered Renée, intrigued by where Madison was going.

"Excellent," said Madison, "Get it from your locker and put on the headphones, put on your favorite music and put it up loud. Then lie down on the towel, legs either side of the bench and make yourself come again. Close your eyes and keep them closed. When you are climaxing I will ask you to do something for me."

Renée looked into Madison's eyes and nodded.

As Renée left the shower, Madison spanked her bottom playfully and then followed her out.

Renée bent over and picked up her towel then went to her locker and got her iPod as instructed. She put the headphones into her ears and turned on her exercise playlist, a mix of upbeat French hip hop and pop, and turned it up loud. She then draped the white towel over the bench which was in the center of the room between the two walls of lockers. Renée then went to the door of the change rooms and peaked out. The hallway was empty.

Renée then lay down upon the towel, resting a leg on either side of the bench. With her legs splayed she stroked herself in time with the music. Renée then closed her eyes.

Madison dressed in a skirt and blouse, keeping her eyes on Renée. After a minute or so three women came into the change rooms. They were immediately taken aback by Renée, so wantonly displaying herself in the middle of the change room.

Madison smiled at the women and tilted her head towards Renée and raised her eyebrows.

"She's my friend," said Madison.

"She looks like she's having a good time," said the first woman who watched Renée's chest rise and fall while one of Renée's hands was stroking her nipples while the other one was buried deep between her legs.

"What a tramp," said the second woman sniggering.

"She's quite sexy," said the third woman.

"Touch her," said Madison, "I dare you."

"I'm not touching her," said the second woman.

"She doesn't look like she needs any help," said the first woman.

"It's her fantasy," said Madison, "She wants you to see her. She wants you to touch her."

"Total strangers?" asked the second woman.

"Just touch her leg and you will see," said Madison.

The second woman lightly touched the top of one of Renée's thighs. Renée immediately purred with pleasure.

"How bizarre," said the second woman.

"Twist her nipple," said Madison.

"What?" asked the second woman.

"I'll do it," said the third woman, stepping forward and holding Renee's left nipple between her thumb and finger and twisting the nipple lightly.

"Oh," Renée moaned.

"What a tramp," said the second woman.

"My turn," said the first woman stepping forward and brushing her hand up and down Renée's thighs."

"Oh," Renée moaned again.

"Does she desire everyone who touches her?" asked the first woman.

"Yes," said Madison, "And you know what she likes doing the best?"

"I can't wait," said the second woman.

"Eating women out," said Madison.

The women all giggled.

"Don't laugh," said Madison, "She's very talented. Best tongue in New York."

The women giggled again and Madison kissed Renée on the lips then moved her fingers to Renée's mouth who sucked upon her fingers while still stroking up and down between her legs, pinching her labia together to stimulate her clitoris.

Madison studied the intense look on Renée's face and knew she was a short time away from climaxing.

"Don't you want to have the orgasm of your lifetime?" asked Madison.

"This is crazy," said the second woman.

"I'll try it," said the third woman, yanking up her work skirt and pulling down her panties.

"OK," said Madison, "Now stand astride her face and wait until I tell you to lower yourself down."

"Darlene, you are wild," said the first woman and they all laughed.

"Well I don't want to die wondering," said the third woman.

Madison kissed and stroked Renée cheek and neck. This was enough to send Renée into paroxysms of pleasure.

Madison then nodded to Darlene who lowered herself onto Renée's face. Renée immediately licked and slurped the length of Darlene's labia and then probed between them with her tongue, finding the tip of her opening and alternated between sucking and licking Darlene's clitoris.

Darlene and Renée moaned in unison while the other three women looked on in fascination. Darlene was soon riding Renée's mouth like a horse, bucking forward and backward and grinding into Renée's face.

The two other women stroked Renée's breasts and pulled her nipples while Madison kissed Renée's mouth, swallowing her orgasm when it came.

CHAPTER 9. NIGHTCLUBBING

That evening Madison invited Renée to join her and Sonya to go nightclubbing. Renée wore a glittering blue mini dress that hugged her curves and black stockings which showed off her long shapely legs.

After a number of cocktails, they were relaxed and danced together when Sonya's favorite dance track was played at the club they were in. After that Sonya and Madison sat at the bar watching Renée continue to dance.

"You like Renée?" asked Madison.

"What's not to like," said Sonya.

"She is one of a kind," said Madison.

"I have to admit I think about her," said Sonya watching Renée hips sway to the music, with her eyes closed.

"Nothing wrong with that," said Madison.

"What's she into?" asked Sonya.

"Being an actress she likes being the center of attention."

When Renée returned from the dancefloor she quickly knocked down a cocktail.

"What's say you and Madison, join me for cocktails at my apartment. I live just around the corner from here. I have amazing views of the water," said Sonya.

"Just one cocktail and then we better get home," said Renée, "I've got work tomorrow."

"Me too," said Sonya.

After leaving the club the group caught a taxi for the short distance to Sonya's building. Sonya rested her hand on Renée's thigh.

The view from Sonya's apartment was amazing. It looked over the deep blue of the Hudson River with the skyscraper lights twinkling over the water.

Sonya had decorated her walls with extra-large black and white photographs of women's bodies in close up so that they looked like landscapes.

"My former girlfriend took those," said Sonya, gesturing to the photographs.

"Are any of them you?" asked Renée.

"You have to compare and contrast to work out which one is me," said Sonya playfully.

The group settled into a large black plush corner lounge suite where Sonya served her guests drinks from her bar.

On the lounge, Madison moved her hand along Renée leg, up her dress and all the way to the top of her thigh and kissed her softly on her lips.

"You look amazing," Madison said.

"You too," said Renée.

Madison then reached the top of Renée's panties and pulled them down along her legs and over her black high heeled shoes.

"We don't need these do we, Renée?" Madison whispered in Renée's ear.

"No but I don't want to be the only one in the room with a bare butt," said Renée kissing Madison's cheek softly, like a butterfly against a flower.

Madison then turned to Sonya and kissed along her neck, with Sonya leaning her head back against the soft black leather of the couch.

Sonya closed her eyes as Madison expertly caressed the back of her head, making her almost swoon just by massaging her scalp.

Madison then spread her legs so that one leg was over Renée and one leg was over Sonya and pulled Sonya's head down between her legs.

"Come over here, madam," said Madison.

Sonya kissed Madison's pubic hair then kissed either side of her inner thighs.

"I love your kissing," said Madison, pulling her labia apart with her fingers, "I want you to kiss me there."

Sonya's cheeks blushed as her tongue probed deep within Madison.

Madison then unbuttoned her blouse and removed her bra then looked pointedly at Renée who immediately turned her attention to Madison's breasts, licking and sucking her nipples while Sonya's tongue was buried deep within the folds between Madison's legs.

Madison ground herself against Sonya's tongue, riding her face slowly and deeply.

Renée then ran her tongue over Madison's nipples while using her hands to cup each of her breasts.

Madison then noticed a thick book of modern photography on the glass top table in front of them.

"You both have delicious kisses but I wonder which of you has the best deportment," said Madison.

Sonya and Renée both straightened up and looked at Madison who said, "Both of you stand up and remove your clothes but leave your high heels on."

Soon both Sonya and Renée were naked before Madison, wondering exactly what Madison meant by deportment.

"Sonya, place that book on your head and walk across the room to the window," said Madison, pointing to the window with a riding crop which she pulled from her handbag.

"I...I don't have very good balance," said Sonya who was not often lost for words.

"Stand up," Madison said abruptly.

Sonya stood up, naked before Madison.

"Head up, Sonya," said Madison tapping her chin with the riding crop.

Sonya adjusted the position of her head.

"This won't do," said Madison, pointing the riding crop at each of Sonya's nipples.

"I'm sorry. I don't understand," said Sonya looking down at her chest.

"Your nipples should be redder. Go to your handbag and apply your lipstick to your nipples and play with them to make them firmer," Madison said pointing the tip of the riding crop at each nipple.

"Yes, I will," said Sonya going to her handbag and getting her lipstick out, pulling and caressing her nipples until they stiffened and then applied the bright red lipstick to them.

Renée could not help but feel aroused by watching Sonya as she readied herself for whatever Madison meant by deportment.

"And apply the lipstick to your labia as well," said Madison.

"Yes, Madison," said Sonya.

"Is that the name you should call me by?" asked Madison.

"I..I don't even know your full name," said Sonya.

"I want you to call me mistress," said Madison.

"Yes, mistress," Sonya said, her head bowed.

"Now get to work," said Madison harshly.

Sonya sat and applied the lipstick between her legs so that her labia, nipples, and mouth were all the same bright shade of red.

Madison inspected Sonya's application of the lipstick, "Good girl."

"Now stand up straight," said Madison.

"Yes, mistress."

Madison then picked up the book from the coffee table and balanced it on Sonya's head.

"Now walk to the window and back," said Madison, "If it falls then you will be punished."

"Punished? How so?"

"I am the one who asks the questions and makes the demands. Is that understood?" said Madison, moving the riding crop up along the inside of Sonya's leg.

"Yes, mistress," said Sonya, the book heavy upon her head.

Sonya was completely out of her comfort zone but was being driven by some strange inner compulsion to submit. She had never been naked like before. It felt so wrong but deliciously dangerous at the same time.

Sonya walked step after step towards the window. Her heels were very high and the book threatened to fall from her head with every step. She reached the window and looked out at the Hudson River and the city lights against the water.

"Stay there for a moment," said Madison who walked over to Sonya and kissed the back of her neck and then drew the riding crop down the back of the neck and down her spine then patted it across each cheek of her buttocks.

"Good girl," said Madison, "Now Renée..."

"Yes, mistress," said Renée.

"Lie down with your head resting on the side of this sofa with your legs apart and caress yourself," said Madison.

Renée smiled slightly. She did not know where Madison was going with this but she knew it was going to be wild. With her head leaned backward on the armrest of the sofa, Renée draped one leg over the top of the sofa and the other on the floor and moved two fingers up and down between her legs.

"Sonya, now you walk back here to the sofa, making sure to keep the book balanced on your head and lower yourself onto Renée's head," Madison said.

In her mind, Sonya was saying *what?* Nonetheless, Sonya walked back from the window, her hips and breasts swaying as she walked in the high heeled shoes, her head very straight, being careful not to drop the book, balanced precariously on her head. As Sonya approached Renée she drank in her beauty and her erotic display and it made her feel weak at the knees and she almost lost her composure. Sonya moved one leg either side of Renée's face and soon felt the smoothness and warmness of Renée's tongue caressing between her legs. Sonya closed her eyes momentarily, savoring the intense pleasure she was experiencing.

"Good girls," Madison said, moving the riding crop down Sonya's side, "Renée move your head up more and try and reach your tongue more deeply into Sonya."

Sonya immediately felt Renée's tongue moving back and forth more intensely then her legs started to shudder involuntarily as she climaxed, the book tumbling from her head and caught by Madison.

"Did I tell you to drop the book?" Madison said harshly.

Sonya did not respond immediately, lost in her orgasm.

"Sorry, mistress," Sonya whispered.

"Go to the balcony and hold the railing," Madison said.

Sonya looked at Renée so tender and beautiful. The expression on her face was one of regret. She said softly "sorry," as Sonya walked to the balcony railing, her head bowed.

"Bottom higher in the air," said Madison.

Sonya looked out at the river and wondered if anyone on the passing ferry could see her as Madison rained down three quick whips of the riding crop upon Sonya's bare buttocks.

"What do you say, Sonya?"

"Thank you, mistress."

"Stay there," said Madison.

Madison then walked to the top drawer on a chest of drawers and pulled out a large black strap on double-headed dildo. She then undid her skirt and removed her underwear and eased the dildo into herself and strapped it around her waist.

Renée watched Madison intensely as she continued to stroke herself, even more aroused than she was before. The dildo stood out almost obscenely out from Madison's slim frame

"Sit up Renée," said Madison, "Wrap your lips around this."

Renée sat up on the sofa but continued to stroke herself as she moved her mouth up and down over the head of Madison's dildo as Madison moved the tip of the riding crop from the middle of Renée's back to the nape of her neck. Madison then turned around to check that Sonya was still bent over, holding the balcony railing, her legs impossibly long in high black heels and her bare buttocks showing the three red lines of the riding crop.

Madison then felt the warm hands of Renée upon her buttocks as Renée pulled her nearer, trying to consume more of the large black dildo. Madison rocked her hips slightly as Renée's head was bobbing up and down upon the dildo, making loud slurping noises.

"Good girl, Renée," said Madison. When Sonya heard this she could not help but feel insanely jealous.

This comment also prompted Renée to work even harder at sucking upon Madison's dildo, taking as much of it within her mouth and throat as possible and stroking up and down the back of Madison's legs with her hands.

"Sonya, get over here," said Madison.

"Yes, mistress," said Sonya.

"Bend over and hold onto the top of the sofa," said Madison.

As Sonya walked she saw Renée stroking herself and engorging herself upon Madison's dildo. Sonya held the top of the sofa and Madison roughly handled Sonya's buttocks and then parted them, running her fingers up and down between Sonya's legs.

Madison then pulled the dildo away from Renée's mouth and pushed into Sonya, penetrating her slightly then with each thrust went deeper until he was so deep into her that he almost lifted her feet off the floor.

"Renée, keep stroking yourself but stand up and lick my nipples," said Madison.

"Yes, mistress," said Renée who then unbuttoned Madison's blouse as Madison continued to thrust into Sonya. Renée then removed Madison's bra and sucked upon her dark nipples.

Sonya sighed with each thrust of Madison's dildo into her. Madison tapped Sonya's thigh with the riding crop as if she was riding a horse.

CHAPTER 10. JUDGE

The following day Madison was due to meet Anja at Anja's office so they could meet prior to going to court for the first day of the trial. Anja was concerned as Madison was running late for the meeting and checked her telephone. There were no messages from Madison.

'Where are you?" texted Anja.

After a short time came back the text - "What are you doing?"

"You're late," replied Anja.

Madison sent back an emoji yawning.

"This is serious. Court starts at 10 am," Anja texted back.

"Touch yourself," Madison texted back.

"No," texted Anja in reply.

"You know you want to," texted Madison.

"I want you to attend our meeting," texted Anja.

"I'll come to the meeting if you touch yourself now," texted Madison.

Anja did not reply and looked around the office but no one was looking at her.

"Go on," texted Madison.

Anja looked around the office again. Everyone was quietly working or talking on the telephone. Anja discretely moved her hand to her thigh and moved her hand up and down along it.

"Done," replied Anja by text.

"Good girl," replied Madison by text, then the following words appeared on Anja's phone, "Take a photo."

Anja looked around the office. Still, no one was paying her attention and the managing lawyer was on the far side of the office.

Anja turned the flash on her telephone off and took a quick selfie, smiling down into the camera. She checked the photo before texting it to Madison.

"Beautiful," replied Madison then texted, "Something more intimate?"

Anja looked around the office again. The coast was still clear. She unbuttoned the first couple of buttons of her blouse and took another selfie, moving her lips together in an air kiss expression. Anja then texted the photo to Madison.

"Getting me hot," texted Madison.

Anja looked around the office again while discretely buttoning up her blouse.

"Something more?" Madison texted.

Anja looked around. No one was looking at her and her boss was still on the other side of the floor.

Anja then moved the camera under her desk and slightly spread her legs to take the next photograph. She looked around the room again before checking the photograph. It was so dark you could barely tell what it showed. Anja decided to text it to Madison anyway.

"Wow," Madison texted back, "I'm in the lift. Make sure you are nice and wet for me."

Anja hesitated before replying then chose a smiley face emoji to reply.

Anja was startled when her office telephone started to ring.

"Hello?"

"Ms. Fabre is here to see you."

"Thank you."

Anja was surprised at the outfit that Madison was wearing when she saw her in reception. Madison looked stunning but it was not the usual attire clients wore for court and she started to wish she had given Madison her usual talk to clients about what to wear for court.

In the conference room, Madison just smiled and kept her eyes on Anja. She did not have the pre-trial nervousness that clients ordinarily exhibited. Madison was remarkably calm for someone about to have a seven-day trial.

Anja took Madison through the order of witnesses and what would happen at different parts of the trial. Madison looked bored and stood up and walked to the large windows on one side of the conference room. Anja could see that Madison was naked under her clothing which was transparent in the sunlight.

Madison yawned.

"You don't seem concerned in the slightest," Anja said.

"Why should I be concerned I have the brightest most beautiful attorney in all New York," said Madison.

Anja did not see Madison look concerned at all until she saw the judge in the courtroom who would be presiding over her case.

Judge Chiara Barossa was notorious for being difficult and bad-tempered. Anja, of course, had warned Madison about the judge in the taxi to court but nothing Judge Barossa was much more formidable than expected. She looked at Madison sternly when the charge was read - conspiracy to commit forced labor and Madison pleaded to it.

Poor Sonya thought Madison. Firstly she had the shock of realizing that she had drawn Judge Barossa for the trial and then she looked like she would pass out when she cast eyes on Madison and realized that Madison was the accused on trial.

Madison could read Sonya's thoughts as she tossed over declaring a conflict of interest and having to organize a new prosecutor but there would be awkward explaining to do and Madison had calculated correctly that Sonya would keep her connection to Madison under wraps and would not disqualify herself.

This Judge Barossa would be a tougher nut to crack, thought Madison and there was not much time to do it. Judge Barossa seemed to treat everyone with contempt and took delight in belittling and intimidating everyone in the courtroom.

I bet she loves being dominant in her sex life, thought Madison.

The first witness was Helena Caddell, a model who worked for Madison as a concierge at Madison's famous and decadent women-only parties held at her mansion.

"I thought they were fun... at first," said Helena from the witness box, "But then they became too risqué."

"Can you elaborate please Ms. Caddell," Sonya said.

"Well, at first Madison wanted me and the waitresses to wear little black dresses, black stockings, and black high heels," said Helena, "Which was fine. But then she held parties with different themes and the costumes she got us to wear sometimes went too far."

"Yes?" said Sonya.

Anja could see that the jury was already wondering what was in store for them with this trial.

"Well, we had a Greek toga party where Madison insisted that the waitresses and I be naked under our togas. The togas were no thicker than bed sheets and then Madison and her friends thought it would be enormous fun to spray me with champagne."

"I spent half the night in a wet toga dress that clung to me like a wet T-shirt," said Helena, "And another time Madison held a "maids and mistresses party" where the waitresses and I had to wear ridiculously short maid dresses. Every time we bent over to serve a drink the dress would rise up showing the frilly white panties that came with the outfit."

"Yes," said Sonya.

"The worst party was towards the end, just before I told Madison I was not prepared to work for her anymore. We all had to wear short pleated skirts and white blouses with no underwear at all. Madison's friends made comments about us all night. They made very personal comments."

"What option, if any, did you have to participate in this?" Sonya asked.

"I had none," replied Helena.

"Thank you, Ms. Caddell, that's all the questions I have," said Sonya.

"Ms. Sonnen, your witness," the Judge said.

"Ms. Caddell, you were paid good money to be the hostess at Ms. Fabre's parties, is that right?" asked Anja.

"In the beginning, yes," said Helena.

"And then you agreed to participate in the parties for free," said Anja.

"I stopped being paid," said Helena.

"That was because you enjoyed serving Ms. Fabre and her friends."

"I did not enjoy it. I was embarrassed by how they treated me," said Helena.

"Then why did you attend each party for months after you stopped being paid?" asked Anja.

"She has a way about her. She is very good at manipulating people," said Helena, staring directly at Madison who looked back and slightly smiled.

"You were not threatened or promised anything were you for attending these parties?" Anja said.

"No," said Helena.

"You attended each party after you stopped being paid," said Anja.

"Yes."

"You followed the instructions you were given," said Anja.

"Yes."

"Ms. Fabre provided you with food, drink, and entertainment. Is that correct?"

"Yes, if you can call what happened at her parties entertainment," said Helena.

"You never raised a word of complaint?"

"No...I," Helena seemed lost for words.

"No further questions, Your Honor," said Anja.

"Any re-examination?" the Judge asked Sonya.

"No, Your Honor," said Sonya.

CHAPTER 11. CELEBRATION

Madison was very pleased with how the first day of her trial had gone and bought Anja dinner at Savoureux which after-hours became a hip bar and restaurant. In the taxi, on the way to the restaurant, Madison leaned over to Anja and said, "You must give yourself randomly. Anything that can be desired must be expected. Do you understand."

Anja nodded and said quietly, "Yes, mistress."

Renée was waitressing that night at Savoureux and greeted Madison and Anja with a big grin, "Bonsoir, Madison and who is your friend?"

"Anja Sonnen, pleased to meet you," Anja shook hands with Renée.

"Renée Mercier. Pleased to meet you too."

"Renée, what time do you finish work tonight?" Madison asked.

"At ten."

"I was hoping you and Anja could help me at my store tonight," said Madison.

"Yes, no problem," said Renée.

"Help you at your store? I have to prepare for court tomorrow," said Anja.

"It won't take long," said Madison mysteriously.

At ten, after dining on ratatouille niçoise and quiche and French wine the group walked a few blocks to the local shopping district. The streets buzzed with taxis and the sidewalks were full of shoppers taking advantage of the latest sales.

"In here," Madison said, gesturing to head into a luxury lingerie store with large windows displaying mannequins in the latest ornate underwear and stockings with a rich red curtain behind them like from an old theatre.

"Well hello Madison," said an immaculately dressed older woman with long stocking-clad legs and deep red lipstick, "And who do we have here?"

"Catherine, this is Renée, an actress, and Anja, a lawyer, our models for tonight," said Madison.

Catherine shook hands with everyone and looked Anja and Renée up and down, "Yes, they are perfect. I have just the lingerie for them."

"What?" said Anja, "I thought you said this would take a minute."

"Don't worry," said Madison.

Madison settled into a plush red velvet settee while Catherine took Anja and Renée to the changerooms.

"I have something perfect for the two of you," said Catherine, patting them gently on their bottoms as they walk.

"What is happening here tonight?" asked Anja.

"I am organizing some publicity for this store which Madison owns and I run and you are going to be the star attractions," Catherine said.

"Yes? Tell us more," said Anja.

"You don't have to worry about anything. I'll explain it all as we go along. First, get out of your clothes and hang them over the chairs over there and come over to the washbasin," Catherine said.

There was a 1950's white porcelain pedestal basin at the back of the room with a small circular mirror above it. Next to it were two old kitchen chairs. Renée stripped effortlessly. Her body a work of art.

With some trepidation, Anja removed her clothes, underwear, and shoes and waited for her next instruction.

"OK Renée and Anja come closer to the washbasin and stand very still," Catherine said, getting out a cut-throat razor and some shaving cream from a nearby cabinet.

"What's that for?" asked Anja looking anxious.

"We find it helps the appearance of the lingerie," Catherine said, stirring soap with a shaving brush and then applying the brush up and down along Anja's pubic hair.

"Open your legs a little," Catherine said and when Anja had complied, brushed the shaving brush up and down between Anja's legs.

"Come on a little more. We need to get every hair," said Catherine, "Put one leg up on the basin."

Anja was slightly unsteady for a moment before getting her foot up onto the basin, giving Catherine better access between her legs.

Catherine continued to apply the brush forwards and backward between Anja's legs until Anja felt aroused. Anja had to stifle a sigh, the sensation felt so nice, the brush felt very similar to a tongue.

Once the soap lather had been applied Catherine then sharpened the razor on some brown leather and held the blade to the light to inspect the sharpness of it. She sharpened the blade some more and then applied the blade to the inside of one of Anja's thighs and then the other.

"Leg down please," Catherine said then shaved down below Anja's stomach, carefully removing all of her pubic hair. Catherine then washed the remaining soap away and dried with a towel.

"Give me a look," Catherine said, peering very closely at Anja's bare private area and then pushing her nose between the folds of Anja's labia and then grabbed her buttocks and moved her head slightly back to lick up and down between Anja's legs.

"My finishing touch," Catherine said, "Now go next door and see what Madison wants to dress you in. Now Renée you come over here."

When Anja entered the next room Madison unzipped a lingerie bag and produced an exquisite black lace lingerie set barely hanging off a black clothes hanger.

"Ah, where am I going to be modeling this?" Anja asked.

"You'll see. Now try it on. I can't wait to see how it looks on you."

Anja pulled on the black lace panties which were essentially a G string with see-through lace mesh at the front and a black ribbon that met at the top of her bottom.

"The idea is that your lover pulls the ribbon and the panties come loose," said Madison.

Anja then put on the bra and found the cups of the bra were made of the same black mesh with her pink nipples clearly prominent behind the mesh. Instead of a fastener, there was a black ribbon at the back.

"I feel a little exposed," said Anja.

"It's very discrete. You are all covered and decent I assure you," said Madison lying through her teeth.

"Now slip these on," said Madison who opened a shoebox and produced some sky-high shiny black Louboutin stilettos.

Anja almost gasped at how high the shoes were.

"I'll help you get them on," Madison said, "Lift up your foot."

Anja lifted up her foot and Madison held it and sucked upon Anja's toes then slipped the shoe on and strapped it up and then did the same with the other foot, Anja having to steady herself on the basin to avoid toppling over.

"OK let's see you walk," said Madison.

Anja walked the length of the backroom like a newborn giraffe.

"That won't do. You need to walk like this," said Madison, walking high and confidently back and forth across the room, swinging her hips.

Anja tried again, trying to emulate Madison's confidence.

"Mmm. Much better. I could ravish you right here all night but you have work to do," said Madison.

Anja began to get concerned that she would soak right through the flimsy panties.

"You still haven't told me where you want me to model," Anja said.

"Before I do that, just one more touch," said Madison wrapping a black velvet mask around Anja's eyes and then applying red lipstick to Anja's lips and putting an earpiece in her ear.

"Now all you need to do is go through this door over here and dance to the music. I will give you further instructions over the earpiece including when it's time for you to return," Madison said guiding Anja out through a door that led to a long corridor.

Anja felt her way and opened the door at the end of the corridor and felt a velvet curtain. She pulled where the curtains joined each other aside and passed through.

Anja breathed in quickly and was startled, she went back behind the curtain and tried the door behind her but it had locked.

Music started on the speaker fixed to the ceiling.

Anja was in the front shop display area reaching her hands out to try and get her bearings.

"Relax Anja," Madison's voice could be heard from the speaker.

Anja steadied herself. None of the shoppers seemed to be giving her too much attention as they rushed by.

"Dance," said Madison.

"Yes mistress," said Anja who closed her eyes and started to sway her hips to the music.

People from the street started to stop and watch Anja. Some of the shoppers put their hands on the glass. Some almost trip over while watching Anja and walking by. A businesswoman stood in front of the glass and blew a kiss to Anja.

"Blow a kiss," Madison said over the speaker.

Anja blew a kiss.

The businesswoman traces Anja's shape on the glass.

"Smile," Madison said.

Anja smiled.

"Stroke the sides of your breasts," said Madison.

Anja hesitated.

"Do it now," said Madison.

Anja lifted her arms up and then stroked the side of each breast with the back of her hand. Anja could not help but become aroused, her nipples almost poking through the mesh of the bra.

"Sit on the chair," Madison said over the speaker.

Anja sat on the one chair in the display area. The wood was cold against her bottom.

"Now interlock your fingers between your legs and spread your legs wide," said Madison.

Anja interlocked her fingers and brought her hands down in front of her crotch then moved one leg out and then the other.

The crowd stirred. Some women dragged their men along the street. The businessman looked like he was going to collapse. Then there was the flash of someone taking a photograph and then another and another. A journalist was interviewing people in the street.

"Stand up and turn around and bend down and hold your ankles," said Madison.

Anja followed the instructions and reached down, her buttocks directed at the crowd. She then moved her hands down each side, past her hips and kept going down until she reached her calves.

"Just hold it there," said Madison into the earpiece.

"Wiggle your bottom," said Madison.

Anja followed the instruction, wiggling her bottom so that her buttocks jiggled. Some of the crowd had their faces pressed up to the glass trying to get a better view of Anja.

"Now stand up and dance in time to the music," Madison said.

Anja danced, swaying her hips and arms.

When the music ended Madison said, "Now bow."

Anja stood where the curtains met by the doorway and bowed, the crowd fixated on Anja's cleavage.

Anja then felt a movement behind her and the curtain move slightly and then there was something pressing up against her between her legs.

"Don't move," Madison said over the earpiece.

Anja then felt herself being penetrated from behind.

"It's me Renée."

Not knowing what to do, Anja remained bent over as Renée thrust into her, making Anja's breasts sway forwards and backward as Renée pulsed in and out of her.

The crowd was enormous now. Renée could see the lights of a television camera crew and a cameraman filming them. Then to one side, Renée saw two police officers heading towards the store.

"Anja, the cops are here. Let's go," hissed Renée who then quickly disappeared behind the curtain.

Anja quickly moved behind the curtain and then removed her blindfold, "I can't get arrested. I'm an attorney"

Reya ran, her strap on dildo slapping her in the stomach as she went.

Madison was sitting in front of a CCTV display laughing madly.

"This way," said Catherine, handing them coats and holding a back door open. Anja, Madison, and Renée disappeared down an alley and into a waiting car.

The car disappeared into the stream of traffic, leaving Catherine to explain to the police that she did not know what the models were doing in the shop window. The police searched the store before disbursing the crowd who were all hoping for a further glimpse of the two beautiful models.

CHAPTER 12.
SERVICE

Madison gave Renée and Anja long coats to wear and directed the car to go to an expensive-looking apartment block.

"Let her know they have arrived," said Madison to the driver and then turned to the two women and said, "Anja keep the earpiece in your ear and follow my instructions."

"Where are we going?" asked Anja.

"Just follow my instructions," said Madison.

"Will this take long. I need to get some sleep before court tomorrow," said Anja.

"Not long," said Madison who then handed each woman a pink studded collar with a bell at the front with the bell containing a small camera.

"What are these?" asked Renée.

"Just put these on and when you arrive follow Anja's lead. I will tell her what to do. I promise it will be fun," said Madison.

The women attached the collars around their necks.

"Renée, now connect this to Anja's collar," said Madison handing Renée a bright pink lead.

Madison then turned to Anja and said, "Now Anja put your blindfold back on."

A large metallic door opened and the car drove in and stopped near a lift. The lift doors opened and there was a maid who waved to the car.

"Renée, take the lead and follow that woman. I will collect you when you are finished," said Madison.

Renée walked to the maid leading Anja by the bright pink lead. The dildo pressed forwards against the cloth of the long coat she was wearing. The maid did not even raise an eyebrow. She had seen everything as her employer had very particular tastes on the wild side of life.

"Quite cool tonight," said the maid, making small talk on the way up to the penthouse.

Renée and Anja nodded.

"Evening ladies," Anja heard an older woman's voice that sounded so familiar to her.

"Bonsoir," said Renée.

"I love your accent," said the woman, "Please come in."

Anja recognized the voice with shock. It was Judge Chiara Barossa. Anja shuddered with fear.

Meanwhile, the Judge admired the gentle sway of the bottoms of the two women as they walked into her apartment.

"Can I get you ladies something to drink?" the Judge asked.

"Non, merci," said Renée.

Anja just shook her head.

"Does she speak?" asked the Judge.

"No. She does not know any English," Renée ad-libbed.

"French as well?"

"Oui," nodded Renée.

"I like your jewelry," said the Judge.

Renée looked down and did not realize what the Judge was talking about and then realized it was the collars that the two women wore that the Judge was referring to.

"Can I take the lead?" the Judge asked and Renée handed the Judge the bright pink lead.

"Drop your coat and get down on your hands and knees," said Madison into Anja's earpiece.

Anja shrugged off her coat and sunk to the floor, wishing for a moment that the earth would just swallow her up as she felt so embarrassed. Renée also removed her coat, revealing the large black strap on dildo that rose up from her midsection. The Judge smiled at the sight of it.

"Hold this," the Judge said to Renée handing her a bottle of whiskey.

The Judge then pulled on the lead and walked Anja around the room as she crawled on her hands and knees. Renée stared at Anja. The Judge then stopped and sat on the sofa. Anja remained on the floor in front of her. The Judge ran her hand over Anja's head and stroked the back of her neck and then moved her hand over Anja's back and then gently squeezed each of her buttocks.

"Rub yourself against her," said Madison.

Anja then still terrified of being recognized by the Judge rubbed against the Judge's legs with her body.

"Sit up," said the Judge.

Anja knelt on the floor. She felt that surely the gig was up now and that the Judge would recognize her.

"You have beautiful breasts," said the Judge gently squeezing each one in turn and then running her fingers over the top of the soft lingerie, stimulating Anja's nipples until they pressed firmly against the material.

"I like your lips as well," said the Judge, her fingers tracing a circle around Anja's mouth.

"Open your mouth," said Madison.

Anja opened her mouth and the Judge slipped two fingers into Anja's mouth and felt her tongue.

"You have a nice strong tongue. I will put that to good use later," said the Judge, "Now get up onto the sofa next to me with your legs over the top of the sofa."

Anja blindly felt her way to the sofa and lay with her back on the sofa cushion and her head hanging down.

The Judge moved her hands towards the blindfold but before Anja could be unmasked Renée stepped in and said, "Sorry madame. My friend is very shy the blindfold must stay on."

"No bother. Now my sweet one, part your other lips," said the Judge.

Anja used two fingers of her right hand to part her labia.

"Now you take a gulp of the whiskey then remove this one's panties and go down on her," the Judge said.

Renée took a large swig of the whiskey, pulled the ribbon on Anja's panties to remove them and then cupped Anja's buttocks with both hands and licked in a long line between Anja's legs with just the right amount of pressure to make Anja squirm with pleasure. After licking up and down between Anja's legs she then found Anja's bud with her tongue and lightly massaged it, her mouth deliciously warm with the whiskey.

"Keep doing that until your friend comes. I want her to come hard," said the Judge who inspected the area between Anja's legs closely as Anja held the lips of her sex open with two fingers.

The Judge cupped each of Anja's breasts and rubbed her nipples between her fingers. Madison placed one finger deep into Anja and lightly caressed her G spot while flicking at Anja's clitoris with her tongue.

"I like your technique," said the Judge.

Anja began to pant and then despite the embarrassing situation, softly sighed as she came.

"Now pour your friend a glass of whiskey," said the Judge, "Put it on the coffee table and guide her to it."

Renée did as the Judge requested.

"Now you bend over the glass of whiskey there and see if you can drink it without holding the glass. Just use your tongue," said the Judge.

Anja bent over the glass of whiskey on the table, was a little unsteady on her high heels for a moment then stuck her tongue into the whiskey glass and lapped at it like a cat, the area between her legs glistened.

"Good kitty," said the Judge stroking Anja's bottom she was stroking a cat.

"And now it's time for you to use that thing you have on," said the Judge to Renée.

"Wiggle your bottom Anja," said Madison into Anja's earpiece. Anja immediately complied.

"Look at her, She's insatiable," said the Judge.

Renée moved the dildo forward so that it pressed up between Anja's pert bottom and penetrated her, reaching her hands around Anja to grab her breasts and moved in and out of Anja with great rigor.

The Judge sat back and sipped from her own glass of whiskey with one hand while spanking Renée's buttocks with her free hand.

At the end of the night, Anja was exhausted and she wondered how she could face the Judge in the morning now that she had tasted her so intimately.

CHAPTER 13. SURRENDER

The next morning Madison caught a taxi with Anja to court.

"The Judge was very happy with you and Renée. She told my driver that she wanted to book you both for Friday night. Of course, he explained that you both would be delighted to see her again," Madison said.

"Really Madison, do you have any sense of decorum at all?" said Anja who still smelt of sex notwithstanding a long hot shower and plenty of perfume.

"Well Anja, you've known me long enough to realize that I follow my own rules," Madison said.

"But Madison there are some lines that if you cross you will not be able to go back from," said Anja.

"I enjoy crossing lines and I think you do too," said Madison, "Everything is a game."

"Well I don't even know how I can face the Judge today," Anja said.

"You'll be fine," said Madison.

The Judge that morning was in a much more agreeable mood than previously in the trial that day. Anja found that she quickly got back into her usual demeanor in court and pushed the events of the night before into the back of her mind.

The first witness of the morning was Antoinette Harrison, Madison's former accountant, a serious-looking woman in her mid-forties with large black-framed glasses which did not suit her face.

"And how did you come to work for free for Ms. Fabre?" Sonya asked Antoinette part of the way through her examination of the witness.

"I just wanted to please her for some reason. Money was no longer important to me," Antoinette said, looking at the jury like a frightened rabbit.

"What services were you providing for Ms. Fabre?" asked Sonya.

"I did the accounts for all of her businesses," replied Antoinette.

"Would you socialize together?"

"Yes, Madison would invite me to her parties."

"What would happen at these parties?"

"They would have different themes. People would dress up."

"Did Ms. Fabre ever get you into a compromising position at these parties?"

"At first... the parties were fun. Well, more than fun – they were the most amazing experience. Then later I came to feel we were all being manipulated by Madison for her own amusement."

"In what way?" asked Sonya.

"I was pushed out of my comfort zone... I had sex with another woman on the dining table at Madison's place while all the other guests watched."

"Why did you agree to that?"

"I don't know. The atmosphere at the party was just so... decadent. Madison created an atmosphere at those parties where anything goes."

"Thank you. No further questions from me."

"Ms. Sonnen?" said the Judge.

"Ms. Harrison, you were the accountant for Ms. Fabre for five years?"

"Yes."

"You attended these parties of your own free will?"

"Yes."

"You were not charging Ms. Fabre for your services prior to the incident where you had sex at a party?"

"That's correct."

"And you were not asked or encouraged by Ms. Fabre to have sex at the party?"

"No, she did not."

"Thank you. Nothing further," said Anja smiling at the Judge. The Judge smiled back which was strange for her. Anja wondered - *was that a smile of recognition?*

At the end of the trial that day Madison invited Anja to La Maison for dinner. Anja could not help but imagine the parties that Madison had conducted at her house.

Madison's maid brought in the food in the large dining room. After dinner, Madison and Anja retreated to an adjourning room where the maid had lit a large wood fire that crackled.

"Is it true that you just manipulate people for your own amusement?" Anja asked as they sat together in a large settee opposite the fire?

"I don't know if amusement is the best word," said Madison stroking Anja's hair, "I truly desire these people. For some people, it gives them pleasure to serve."

"Why do you think all these witnesses are giving evidence against you now?" Anja asked.

"Sometimes people are scared or become scared of their own desires. Also sometimes people get into a group and they can create their own reality or rewrite history," said Madison, "I merely opened the door for people but sometimes people did not like what they saw."

"Can I see the dungeon that is referred to by some of the witnesses?" Anja asked.

"Of course, follow me," Madison said, taking Anja's hand and leading her down a hallway and then downstairs to a basement. The room was warm from central heating and looked like a study with a desk, leather chesterfield couches, and rugs and then Anja noticed a gymnastics mat and bar and a vaulting horse. There were large mirrors on each wall.

"You like to work out?" asked Anja.

"You could call it that," said Madison. "Would you like to try out the equipment?"

"Sure," said Anja.

"See the chest of drawers over there. Go to the top drawer there will be some gym clothes in your size," said Madison.

Anja changed out of her suit and hanged the clothes over a chair.

In the drawer was a pleated skirt and a T-shirt, both of which seemed too small for Anja once she had them on.

"Now lie down on the vaulting horse, one leg either side of it," said Madison.

Anja climbed up on the vaulting horse and lay face down on the padded top of it, her legs splayed on either side.

"You look amazing," said Madison.

"Thank you, mistress," said Anja.

Anja then heard soft buzzing and then felt a vibrator against her panties which Madison kept there until a wet patch on the panties indicated her level of arousal. Madison then massaged that area with her hand, squeezing Anja's labia together and slightly pinching the labia until the panties became even wetter and Anja slightly moaned.

"Push up from the bar with your arms," said Madison.

Anja pushed up and then Madison held Anja's breasts and gripped Anja's nipples tightly between her fingers and pulled upon them.

"Anja, do five push-ups," said Madison.

Madison continued to squeeze Anja's nipples as Anja performed the five push-ups.

"Anja get off the equipment and take off your panties," Madison said.

"Yes, mistress," said Anja, pulling the soaking panties down her legs.

"Now shine my shoes with your panties," said Madison, "Bend down at the waist to do it."

Anja bent down to reach Madison's shoes and rubbed her panties against the leather of Madison's shoes while Madison looked at the raised skirt and round orb of Anja's bottom in one of the mirrors in the basement. Anja's blond hair fell around her head, covering her face. Madison moved her hands onto the softness of Anja's bottom and stroked her buttocks while Anja dutifully shined Madison's shoes.

"I want to review my statement. Can you read it for me?" Madison asked.

"Yes, of course," said Anja.

"It's on the desk over there. Crawl over to it and carry it in your mouth to the rug over there by the chair," Madison said.

Anja was not sure about mixing business with pleasure but nonetheless crawled along the floor, her bottom swaying under the short skirt. When she got to the desk she looked at the papers on the desk and saw Madison's statement. She then picked it up and placed it in her mouth and crawled over to a thick rug next to a brown chesterfield armchair.

"Stay on all fours and put the statement on the ground away so that your bottom is facing the chair," Madison said.

Anja slowly lowered the statement onto the rug with her mouth.

Madison then sat on the chair and admired Anja's pale bottom for a moment.

"Now raise your bottom in the air and read the statement to me," said Madison.

Anja started reading the statement, "I, Madison Lam Fabre, state that all the allegations made against me are..."

It was then that Anja felt the cold leather of Anja's shoe between her legs.

"Rock back and forth upon my shoe as you read please," said Madison.

Anja moved back and forward against the shoe and continued reading "...are false."

Anja then felt Madison's hands on her buttocks again. This time Madison gripped them and moved Anja forward and back more rapidly against the shoe.

"All of my interactions..." Anja had to stop for a moment due to the intensity of the feelings she was experiencing. Immediately she felt the slap of Madison's hand upon her buttock.

"Did I tell you to stop reading or to orgasm?" Madison said harshly.

"No, mistress," said Anja.

"You will only stop reading or orgasm when I tell you."

"Yes, mistress."

"Now turn around and face me and lower yourself onto my shoe," said Madison.

Madison moved a footrest in front of her and placed her feet upon it. Anja moved one leg either side of the footrest and lowered herself down upon Madison's foot so that her labia pressed against the cold leather of the shoe, leaving slight wetness upon it, and continued reading, "...were entirely consensual and of mutual benefit...".

"Please bounce upon the shoe as you read," said Madison.

"Yes, mistress," said Anja moving her legs so that he body went up and down upon the shoe, the tip of the shoe penetrating Anja as she reads the statement.

It was hard to explain but Anja felt great beauty in serving Madison's instructions in this way even though she knew it was not pretty. It was as if two pieces of a jigsaw puzzle were interlocking, revealing a beautiful scene, revealing a wholeness.

CHAPTER 14.
MASK

On the Friday of that week, Anja was Madison's guest at a masked ball held at the luxurious residence of one of Madison's oldest friends, Kathie Lee Berrie. The theme of the party was *Femme and Domme* and Madison assisted Kathie Lee to develop the guest list.

Madison's driver drove Renée to collect the Judge and drive her to the party. Renée wore a black velvet mask, a short sheer black dress that Madison had bought for her, black panties and stockings and high heeled black shoes.

The sky that night was clear and full of stars.

"Well hello gorgeous," the Judge said upon seeing Renée, her beautiful breasts pressing against the sheer dress.

The Judge wore a 1920's style suit with her grey hair slicked back like an old movie star. As they rode to the party, the Judge stroked Renée's thigh firmly like it belonged to her.

Sonya immediately recognized the Judge as she walked into the party even though the Judge wore a black velvet mask and also recognized Renée, walking beside her masked with a gold necklace around her neck that linked with a long gold chain that the Judge held. Sonya felt a mixture of jealousy and self-consciousness. Sonya was dressed in a gold Venetian carnival mask and wore black trousers, black high heels and large black suspenders attached to her pants strategically placed over her breasts to cover her nipples.

An all-women jazz band played in the corner of the ballroom, dressed in black lingerie, masks, stockings and suspenders, and black high heels. The music had a Weimar Republic swing to it. The vocalist with a deep smoky voice crooned songs from Kurt Weill and Tin Pan Alley accompanied by double bass, saxophone, guitar and the rat a tat of a snare drum.

Madison made a dramatic entry. She wore a shimmering sequined flapper's dress with a matching sequined masquerade mask that covered her face. Anja walked beside her with a flapper costume mask with cat whiskers, with a short slinky silk flapper dress that fell upon her curves with black stockings and heels.

"Ladies, our queen has arrived," the vocalist from the jazz band announced when she saw Madison and the crowd erupted into clapping. Madison laughed and bowed to the crowd.

"Let the party begin," Madison shouted to the crowd.

The band immediately launched into a fast swing version of Mack the Knife.

"Let's dance," Madison said to Anja and they joined the crowd dancing the balboa, lindy hop, and charleston. Nearby the Judge danced with Renée.

The next song was slower, a tango. The pianist picks up and plays a bandolean whose music soars over the other instruments in a sensuous melody. Madison held Anja close as they danced, Anja appreciating the closeness with Madison and the way she steers her amongst the couples.

Waitresses dressed in black lace and fishnets like 1920's candy and cigarette girls mingle amongst the crowd with black trays containing glasses of champagne. Madison grabs a glass of champagne for Anja and then another for herself. The singer on stage sings "Dancing in the Moonlight".

"Go up the stairs to the first room on the right," Madison whispered into Anja's ear, "There is a balcony in that room. Lean over the balcony and lift your dress with one hand and stroke yourself with your other hand. Wait there and do not look behind."

Madison watched Anja's behind as it swayed sensuously as she walked up the broad marble staircase to the first floor. When Anja had disappeared she walked over to Sonya.

"You look beautiful," Madison said greeting Sonya by kissing her on each cheek.

Sonya smiled, "I really don't know what I am doing here."

"You've come here to have fun," said Madison, "I have a present for you. Go upstairs to the first room on the left. The present is on the bed."

"Yes, well I hope it is not something illegal. You have got me in enough hot water," said Sonya.

"Don't worry. Nothing like that," said Madison with a half-grin.

Madison watched Sonya walk up the stairs, her breasts swaying with each step underneath the black suspenders. When Sonya had disappeared up the stairs, Madison then walked over to the Judge and Renée who were sipping champagne outside watching the couples dance.

"Good evening ladies. There is something very special happening in the first room on the right upstairs if you would like to see," said Madison.

"Why not?" said the Judge.

"No need to knock," said Madison.

"I see," said the Judge.

Renée took the Judge's hand as they walked up the stairs. Renée opened the door and saw that there were two large glass doors that were open to a large balcony with a beautiful view of the city lights in front of them. There also was a figure leaning over the balcony. Anja held her dress up with one hand and with the other hand, she stroked between her legs.

Renée and the Judge sat at the end of a large bed with a cover embossed with an intricate pattern which was very soft to touch. The Judge noticed how Anja's satin panties were wet where she was stroking them.

Renée removed the Judge's jacket and folded it neatly over a chair and then unbuttoned the Judge's crisp white shirt then kissed the tops of her breasts above her bra with soft kisses. The Judge curled her hand around the back of Renée's neck and stroked it while keeping her eyes transfixed on Anja in the moonlight.

Meanwhile, Sonya was in another room in the mansion looked at a gift-wrapped box in the middle of a large bed with a white linen bedspread. She could hear the sounds of the party below but it almost felt like she was in another world. Sonya sat on the bed and unwrapped the box which was heavier than she expected. Sonya undid the bow and unwrapped the present. There was a white envelope on top of a wooden box.

Sonya opened the envelope and read the card. Madison had written in her elegant handwriting a quote "A gift for my dearest Sonya. I am sure you will put it to good use. M."

When Sonya opened the wooden box she initially did not recognize the object inside. She pulled the object out and realized it was an intricately crafted antique wooden dildo. Underneath it was another note in Madison's handwriting – "Go to the room on your right. You will be able to use your new toy there."

Sonya opened the door of the bedroom she was in and checked that the hallway was clear and then went to the neighboring room. Inside she saw Renée kneeling on the floor in front of the Judge, one hand was stroking one breast while her tongue was licking the other. Sonya then saw Anja leaned over the balcony with one hand holding up her dress while the other stroked between her legs. Sonya sensed someone else in the room and peered into the darkness of one corner of the room and saw Madison's eyes shining through her mask.

Sonya looked to her hand and saw the dark wooden phallus. She then walked over to Anja and grabbed the top of Anja's panties and pulled them down so that they were halfway down her legs. Downstairs the singer is singing "A Pretty Girl Is Like a Melody."

"Put it in her," Madison said.

Sonya eased the end of the dildo into the mouth of Anja's sex and slide it in.

"Now you kneel behind her and suck on the other end. Move it in and out of her with your mouth," said Madison.

Renée picked up a pillow from the bed and placed it on the floor behind Anja and then Sonya knelt on it and wrapped her mouth around the end of the dildo.

"Renée, you also lean over the balcony and present your bottom," Madison said.

Renée sauntered over to the balcony in her high black heels and stood next to Anja and slowly bent over the balcony, her short sheer dress riding up over her buttocks clad in lacy black panties.

"Ms. Barossa, would you be kind enough to help Renée remove her panties?" purred Madison.

The Judge stood up transfixed by the perfect peach presented in front of her. She placed a hand on each of Renée's buttocks and squeezed.

Renée turned around and faced the Judge and flashed a bright smile. Renée was wearing a ruby red lipstick that night. The Judge then slipped her hand between Renée's legs and moved two fingers along the cleft between Renée's legs, over the panties then grabbed the panties and yanked them down and spanked Renée's bottom twice, once on each buttock. Renée released a small gasp in shock.

"Very good, Ms. Barossa," Madison said.

The Judge tapped on each of Renée's inner thighs to get Renée to open her legs wider and ran two fingers up and down upon her labia until they started to moisten.

"Tell Ms. Barossa what you feel Renée en français," Madison said.

"I feel picotements," said Renée.

"What does that mean?" asked the Judge.

"She likes it," said Madison.

The Judge continued to run her fingers up and down the length of Renée's labia while Sonya moved the wooden phallus in and out of Anja with her mouth.

Anja and Renée both looked out at the partygoers below as they simultaneously felt themselves on the brink of orgasm. Suddenly the door of the bedroom opened.

"What the hell is going on here?" it was Kathie Lee Berrie, the owner of the mansion.

Anja and Renée both turned to look in shock and instinctively put their hands over their vaginas in modesty.

Kathie Lee turned the light on in the bedroom and walked over to the balcony. She was wearing a glittering white flapper dress and a mask decorated with peacock feathers.

"Get those hands out of the way and let me have a look at you," she said.

Kathie Lee leaned down so that her face with level with Anja's bottom and spread the cheeks of her arse.

"Hmm, I can see that some monkey business has been going on in my bedroom," Kathie Lee said. She then went over to Renée and spread her buttocks apart and looked at her sex.

Kathie Lee then pushed each woman forward so they were pressed firmly against the edge of the balcony and stood between the women and moved two fingers into each woman and curled them up so that they moved against the G spot of each woman. Anja and Renée had to stand a little more upright and both immediately started to moan in pleasure.

"No one gets up to monkey business in my bedroom without me being involved. Is that understood?" Kathie Lee said harshly.

The Judge and Sonya stood to one side without saying anything, slightly taken aback by the intruder. Anja and Renée just released small cries of pleasure.

Kathie Lee withdrew her fingers from both of them and spanked them with each word she then said, "Is...that...understood?"

Anja sighed, "Oh...yes, mistress."

Then Renée panted, "Oui, madame."

Kathie Lee then turned to Sonya and the Judge and said simply, "Strip and lie side by side on the edge of the bed and play with yourselves."

Kathie Lee then looked over at Madison standing watching in the corner, "And Madison go to my wardrobe and pick out something for these two disobedient young women to wear."

Madison disappeared into the large walk-in wardrobe to the side of the bedroom and came back with two of the cigarette and candy girl costumes that the waitresses were wearing downstairs.

"Good choice," said Kathie Lee who then turned to Anja and Renée and said, "Now ladies, strip but keep your masks and high heels on. Then put on these costumes."

Once the costumes were on they seemed a couple of sizes too short for each woman, the lace tightly hugging each curve of their breasts and barely covering their rear ends.

"Hands behind your backs," said Kathie Lee who was then handed two long pearl necklaces by Madison. Kathie Lee then wrapped one pearl necklace around Anja's wrists and then the other around Renée's wrists.

Kathie Lee then looked closely at the face of each woman and then moved a hand over the breasts of each woman, stroking an caressing them and then pulling on the nipples of each woman in turn until they stood firm and erect against the soft material of the bodice and then pulled each woman by one nipple forward to the bed so that Anja was stood in front of the Judge and Renée in front of Sonya.

"Now you have a contest. The first woman to make their partner come wins the contest and the other will be severely punished," said Kathie Lee haughtily.

Renée and Anja then each lowered themselves to their knees and moved their mouths forward between the legs of Sonya and the Judge. Renée licked up and down Sonya's labia to start with. Anja was more reserved, gingerly pressing her lips against the mouth of the Judge's sex.

Anja heard a whoosh and then felt pain on her buttocks. She looked behind her and Madison held a riding crop aloft and then Anja felt a second strike.

"Madison and I will be encouraging you both. We have a little competition between ourselves and neither of us likes losing," Kathie Lee said, tapping at Renée's buttocks with a riding crop.

Anja nudged her nose between the Judge's labia and then used the bridge of her nose to push against the Judge's clitoris but soon felt the bite of the riding crop against her buttocks again.

Kathie Lee was showing much more reticence about using the riding crop against Renée, instead, she just used it to lift Renée's dress slightly more to admire her buttocks. Sonya's chest was rising and falling more quickly with each caress of Renée's tongue, up and down along her labia.

Anja was having difficulty concentrating with the sting of the riding crop interrupting her progress with getting the Judge off. She then felt Madison's hand pushing the back of her head so that she penetrated the Judge more deeply with her tongue. The Judge made a short murmur of approval but it was too late as Sonya was pulsing with pleasure as Renée pushed her over the cliff of pleasure.

"We have a winner," said Kathie Lee.

Madison removed her hand and Anja looked up at Kathie Lee and Madison, ready to accept her fate.

"And you are the loser," Kathie Lee said to Anja with contempt, "You will now spend the rest of the evening serving my guests," said Kathie Lee hanging a tray around Anja's neck.

Madison put four glasses down then opened a bottle of champagne, the froth spraying upon Anja's bodice and then poured the champagne into the glasses.

"I can't go down to the crowd dressed like this," said Anja in protest, "I don't have any panties on."

"You knew the rules of the game. You're not allowed to wear any panties for the rest of the year," said Kathie Lee.

Anja's face blushed red as she descended the large marble staircase with her hands tied behind her back, the tray in front of her making it hard to see the steps. She felt like everyone at the party was looking at her.

The four glasses of champagne were quickly picked up by the party-goers and Madison replaced those with four more as the band played a rollicking ragtime swing number. When the song finished two of the women dancing came over to Anja and grabbed champagne.

"I love your costume," one of the women said, "Can I touch it?"

The woman ran her hand down the length of Anja's short dress and then onto her thigh and then felt Anja's buttock.

"And no panties?" said the woman, "Scandalous."

"I'm not allowed to wear any panties," said Anja.

CHAPTER 15. NIGHT

Anja traveled with Madison to Madison's home after the party to spend the weekend with her. Anja found the leather of the rear car seat cold against her bare bottom as she sat in the rear of Madison's limousine.

"Kiss me," said Madison from the neighboring seat.

They locked lips for what seemed to Anja like a long time, Madison stroking the sides of her face as they kissed. Anja reveling in their intimacy.

"You pleased me with your devotion," whispered Madison when their lips finally parted and Madison caressed Anja's cheek again with her hand, "Now get out of that dress. I want to see you totally naked."

Anja stripped naked but for her shiny black high heeled shoes.

"Press your breasts against the window," said Madison.

Anja knelt on the seat and then moved her chest forward so that her nipples pressed against the cold glass. Outside the street lights streamed by. Anja almost immediately felt Madison's hand between her legs, circling her clit with two fingers until the fingers were wet. Madison then started to probe Anja's anus with one finger while continuing to stimulate Anja's clit with the other. Anja moaned slightly.

"Now Anja, please sit down and play with yourself," said Madison.

Anja sat back on the cold leather of the limousine seat and parted her legs slightly and started to stimulate herself until her fingers became moist.

"I have something for you because you have done so well to please me this evening," said Madison, showing her a large plastic dildo.

Anja's eyes widened at the size of the dildo as she swirled her hand between her legs.

"Suck it for me," said Madison holding the dildo out.

"Yes, mistress," said Anja nodding obediently.

Anja wrapped her lips around the dildo and moved it back and forward into her mouth and throat while continuing to stroke herself with one hand.

"Look at me when you suck it and let me hear how much you enjoy sucking," said Madison.

Anja nodded and looked Madison directly in her eyes. She could see that Madison was very stimulated by her display. Anja moaned as she sucked.

"Very good, Anja," said Madison who then removed the dildo from Anja's mouth.

One end of the dildo had a suction cup and Madison then stuck the dildo to the limousine window next to Anja.

"Anja, I want you to lick my breasts but I want you to stimulate yourself with the dildo while you do this," said Madison.

Anja hesitated for a moment but she knew that she must follow Madison's instructions. Madison removed her shirt and bra and Anja then knelt on the seat and backed into the dildo so that it penetrated her and then licked and sucked upon Madison's breasts, gently rocking back and forth upon the dildo, making love with the night.

CHAPTER 16. VERDICT

After the limousine arrived at La Maison, Madison held Anja's hand as Anja walked naked from the car to the house and led Anja to her bedroom where Anja removed her heels and got into Madison's large bed. Madison stroked Anja's hair until she fell asleep.

When Anja woke up on Saturday she saw her heels next to a chair where Madison had placed an outfit for Anja to wear which consisted of expensive black lingerie, black stockings, suspenders, a short black dress, and small white apron. Anja went to the adjourning bathroom where Madison had placed a complete set of toiletries, perfume and make up for her use. Anja showered, tied her hair up, applied the makeup and dressed.

When Anja came downstairs Madison was sitting at a table having breakfast overlooking the morning sun in her garden.

"Good morning Anja," said Madison.

"Good morning mistress," said Anja.

"I hope you are hungry. I have had my chef make you fresh croissants this morning."

"Thank you," said Madison, sitting at the table in front of a basket of delicious looking croissants.

"Would you like some coffee?" asked Chloe, entering the room.

"Yes please."

"How do you like it?" asked Chloe.

"Just black please," said Anja.

"Very good," said the chef who quickly returned with dark coffee in a white cup.

The smell of coffee and the sunlight made Anja feel warm.

"What are we going to do today?" asked Anja.

"We are going to have to do something to keep my mind off Monday," said Madison.

"Are you worried?" asked Anja.

"I just want it all to be over now," said Madison.

After they had both finished breakfast Madison and Anja walked upstairs to a large light-filled sitting room with dark hardwood floors and leather sofas and a table and chairs.

"Anja, get a chair and sit in front of me," said Madison sitting down on a sofa.

"Yes, mistress."

Anja picked up the chair and placed it directly in front of Madison.

"Lift your skirt and spread your legs," said Madison, "Then caress yourself."

Anja did as she was asked and Madison just sat there studying each movement Anja made, stroking herself over her panties.

"Does it give you pleasure to follow my instructions?" asked Madison.

"It does, mistress," said Anja.

"Hike your skirt up and lie over my knees," said Madison.

Anja lay over Madison's legs with her bottom facing up. Anja felt Madison's hand on her hair wrapping it in her fingers to lift her head then felt Madison's other hand spank each of Anja's buttocks, causing Anja her to jerk forward.

"Now get down on the floor and kneel at my feet, ready to serve," said Madison.

Anja got down from the sofa and knelt, awaiting further instructions.

"Now lie down on the floor with your legs facing me," said Madison.

Anja lay down in front of Madison so that the heels of her shoes pressed against the sofa on either side of Madison's legs.

Madison stood up and looked down on Anja who she could tell was so eager for her next instruction.

"Legs apart," said Madison.

Immediately Anja spread her legs wide apart. Madison used the front of her foot to caress Madison between her legs.

"Does that give you pleasure?" asked Madison.

"Yes, mistress," replied Anja.

"Rub yourself against my heel," said Madison, placing the heel of her shoe against Anja's crotch.

Anja moved the lower part of her body up and down against the heel.

"Caress your breasts while you do that," said Madison.

"Yes, mistress," said Anja, her cheeks tingling hot.

Anja then stroked her breasts and then pulled upon her nipples over the clothing until they pressed hard against the dress. Anja raised her waist up and down, pushing herself against Madison's heel.

Madison then stepped away from Anja.

"Continue imagining that I am there," said Madison.

Anja continued to caress her breasts and move her waist up and down against the floor.

"Now turn over and kneel upon the floor with your head resting on the floor and your arms behind your back with your wrists next to your ankles," said Madison.

Anja did as she was told, the short dress rising up over her bottom which was presented to Madison.

Madison looked at Anja there so beautiful and compliant.

"Stay there," said Madison who then went downstairs to the kitchen and asked Chloe to bring up two more coffees.

Madison was pleased that Anja had not moved when she returned to the sitting room. When Chloe knocked, Anja had to fight the urge to sit up but remained kneeling on the floor as Chloe placed two coffees on the wooden table next to the sofa where Madison was sitting.

"Is that all, Madison?" asked Chloe.

"Stay with us. Come sit with me," said Madison, patting the sofa seat next to her. Anja felt their gaze upon her. Madison and Chloe then sat and drunk the coffee while discussing Anja and her body as if she was not there.

On Sunday morning Anja caught a taxi to her apartment which for some reason seemed very ordinary and empty after the last two days. Anja could not help but wonder when she could be with Madison again.

On Sunday night Madison could not sleep. She knew that on Monday the jury would be called upon to reach a verdict in her case. Madison telephoned Anja and asked that she stay over at La Maison to keep her company. They had dinner on the terrace of Madison's mansion in the moonlight and then retreated to the loungeroom where Madison played the piano for Anja.

"You play very well," said Anja.

"You are a gracious audience," said Madison.

Anja and Madison traveled by taxi to the courthouse on Monday. They both nodded to Sonya as they entered the courtroom. The Judge looked at the jury intently as she finally addressed them. Anja tried to read what was going through the minds of the jury members but they were inscrutable. When the jury had retired Anja gave Madison a half-smile.

"What will be, will be," Madison said.

The jury was out for a long time.

Madison held her breath while the foreperson announced her verdict, "Not guilty."

Madison hugged Anja.

"Thank you," said Madison.

For the first time, Anja saw tears in Madison's eyes.

Madison opened her handbag and gave Anja a white envelope. When Anja was alone in her apartment she stared at the envelope. Had a drink, looked out at the skyline and then came back to the envelope.

Inside was a plain white card which inside contained a quote in Madison's elegant handwriting, "Thank you for protecting me. Thank you for serving me. Thank you for revealing your secret to me. Thank you for surrendering to me. M."

Anja looked out at the skyline again and smiled to herself, feeling the sunshine with her heart.

Thanks for reading!
Please add a short review on the web-store where you purchased this book and let us know what you thought!

Coming soon
KITTEN
FEMME & DOMME EROTICA 2.
CHAYA CLEMMONS

CHAYA
CLEMMONS
KITTEN
FEMME AND
DOMME EROTICA

For information on hot new releases and a free erotica ebook subscribe to

[1]

•

Don't miss out!

Visit the website below and you can sign up to receive emails whenever Chaya Clemmons publishes a new book. There's no charge and no obligation.

https://books2read.com/r/B-A-QPXI-NUWAB

BOOKS2READ

Connecting independent readers to independent writers.

www.ingramcontent.com/pod-product-compliance
Lightning Source LLC
Chambersburg PA
CBHW071353130726
47996CB00002B/909